THE
RANA LOOK

THE
RANA LOOK

SANDRA BROWN

Bro

THE RANA LOOK

Bantam Loveswept edition / April 1986
Bantam hardcover edition / December 2002

Library of Congress Cataloging-in-Publication Data
Brown, Sandra, 1948–
The Rana look / Sandra Brown.
p.   cm.
ISBN 0-553-10424-1
1. Beauty, Personal—Fiction. 2. Football players—Fiction. 3. Models (Persons)—Fiction. 4. Boardinghouses—Fiction. 5. Businesswomen—Fiction. 6. Texas—Fiction. I. Title.
PS3552.R718 R36 2002
813'.54—dc21   2002071207

Published simultaneously in the United States and Canada

Bantam Books are published by Bantam Books, a division of Random House, Inc. Its trademark, consisting of the words "Bantam Books" and the portrayal of a rooster, is Registered in U.S. Patent and Trademark Office and in other countries. Marca Registrada. Bantam Books, 1540 Broadway, New York, New York 10036.

PRINTED IN THE UNITED STATES OF AMERICA

BVG   10   9   8   7   6   5   4   3   2   1

The
Rana Look

Dear Reader,

You have my wholehearted thanks for the interest and enthusiasm you've shown for my Loveswept romances over the past decade. I'm enormously pleased that the enjoyment I derived from writing them was contagious. Obviously you share my fondness for love stories that always end happily and leave us with a warm inner glow.

Nothing quite equals the excitement one experiences when falling in love. In each romance, I tried to capture that excitement. The settings and characters and plots changed, but that was the recurring theme.

Something in all of us delights in lovers and their uneven pursuit of mutual fulfillment and happiness. Indeed, the pursuit is half the fun! I became deeply involved with each pair of lovers and their unique story. As though paying a visit to old friends for whom I played matchmaker, I often reread their stories myself.

I hope you enjoy this encore edition of one of my personal favorites.

—SANDRA BROWN

One

She met him in the hallway on her way down to dinner.

He was the last kind of surprise she expected. His impact on her was startling. Several things happened at once. She drew in a quick, sudden breath. Her heart slammed into her ribs. She flattened herself against the wall.

"Hi. Did I scare you?" he asked with a smile.

His teeth were white and straight. His easy grin lit up a darkly tanned, weathered face. When his lips tilted up at the corners, one dark brow tipped down, while the other arched high, as though reaching for the wavy lock of sable brown hair that had fallen across his forehead.

It was an intriguing smile. Arresting. Sexy. Her heart was pounding abnormally.

"N-no," she stammered.

"Didn't Aunt Ruby tell you she was getting a new boarder?"

"Yes, but I . . ."

She didn't finish. She couldn't very well say, "Yes, but I pictured a doddering elderly man with a pipe and cardigan, not one whose shoulders practically span the hallway." She had expected the new boarder to have a benevolent face with a pleasant smile. Not one that made her think of daredevils and ne'er-do-wells.

Still smiling, he set down the box of records and tapes he had been holding under his right arm and extended his hand to her. "Trent Gamblin."

Rana stared at his hand for an embarrassing length of time before laying hers against it, not quite clasping it, and muttering, "I'm Miss Ramsey."

When she dared to raise her eyes to his, his smile had deepened. She suspected that he was smiling with derision at her primness.

"Do you need any assistance, Mr. Gamblin?" she asked starchily as she drew her hand back.

"I think I can handle it, Miss Ramsey." His face was solemn now, but the mirth was still twinkling in his eyes. They were the color of coffee liqueur, dark and rich and fluid.

Slightly irked that he apparently found her so amusing, she pried herself away from the wall and stood up straight. "Then if you'll excuse me, I'll go on down for dinner. Ruby gets cross if I'm late for meals."

"Guess I'd better hurry down too. Left or right?"

"Pardon?"

"Which apartment is mine? The one on the left or the one on the right?"

"The left."

"The right one is yours?"

"Yes."

"I sure hope I can keep that straight, Miss Ramsey. I'd hate to come stumbling into your room some night by mistake." His mischievous eyes traveled over her. "No telling what might happen."

He was laughing at her! "I'll see you downstairs," she said coolly. She marched past him, forcing him to press himself up against the wall to let her pass. But he didn't press quite far enough. As she went past him, her clothes dragged against the front of his. He did it on purpose, of course. She could feel his arrogant smile at her back.

If only he knew, she fumed silently as she took the stairs. Miss Ramsey could dazzle him, freeze him in his tracks, wipe that tomcat grin right off his smug face—

Rana paused on the third step from the bottom. Why was she even entertaining such thoughts? She hadn't cared about her appearance for months. All that was behind her. Why now, after meeting the new boarder in Mrs. Ruby Bailey's house, was she even thinking of the Rana she had been six months before?

She disliked herself for it. She had cut herself off completely from her former life. She wasn't ready to resume it, not even temporarily, in order to put the conceited Trent Gamblin in his place.

Becoming the internationally known Rana again would bring back all the self-doubt and pain that went with the single name. She had given up her celebrity status. For the time being she didn't want it back. She was enjoying the anonymity of her current life too much. She liked being simply Miss Ramsey, an undistinguished resident of a typical Galveston boardinghouse.

Ruby Bailey, however, was about as atypical a landlady as one could imagine. When Rana entered the dining room, Ruby was lighting the candles she had placed in the center of the table. In honor of the new arrival, she had gone to special pains with the centerpiece this evening.

"Damn!" she exclaimed, fanning out the match. "I almost caught my nail polish on fire." She inspected the crimson enamel on her nails.

Her age had never been firmly established, but Rana had calculated that it must be beyond seventy, judging from the dated references Ruby occasionally let slip in her colorful dialogue. She was hardly what Rana had pictured when she had responded to the ad in the Houston newspaper advertising an apartment for lease in Galveston.

With the directions Ruby had given her during a brief telephone interview, Rana had located the house without difficulty. Her excitement could barely be contained when she pulled up to the address. The Victorian house, built in Galveston's heyday, had withstood hurricanes as well as the ravages of time. It was situated on a tree-shaded street among other recently restored homes. For Rana, who had lived for the past decade in Manhattan's high rises, it was like stepping into another century. She was delighted. She only hoped she and Ruby Bailey would hit it off.

The landlady's hair was white, but it hadn't been pulled into the classic grandmother's bun, as Rana had imagined. Ruby wore it short and curly, cut in a surprisingly fashionable style. She wasn't matronly plump, either, another misconception on Rana's part, but whipcord lean. Her attire, far from conservative, consisted of a pair of jeans and a sweater the color of the vibrant red geraniums that bloomed in the concrete urns on the front porch.

"You could do with a good meal or two." That blunt statement was the first thing Ruby had said to Rana upon giving her an inspection with busy, no-nonsense brown eyes that could have snapped a longshoreman to attention. "Come on in. We'll start with sugar cookies and herbal tea. Do you like herbal tea? I swear by it. It's good for everything from toothache to constipation. Of course, if you eat the balanced meals I plan on cooking for you, you won't ever be constipated."

And that, it seemed, was that. Ruby considered the apartment on her second floor leased.

Rana would come to learn that Ruby's cup of herbal tea was sometimes liberally laced with Jack Daniel's, especially in the evening after dinner. Rana forgave her friend that particular idiosyncrasy, the same way she forgave Ruby the frown she made no effort to disguise as she looked up now and spotted Rana.

"I was hoping you'd gussy up a bit tonight. Your hair's such a pretty auburn color. Did you ever think of pulling it back away from your face a tad?"

Rana, darling, your cheekbones are to die for! Show them off, love. I see all this glorious hair, sweeping back, big, big volumes of it, like a mane surrounding your face and cascading down your back. Shake your head, darling. See! Oh God, positively to die for! Every tacky little beauty shop in the country will soon be advertising the Rana Look.

Rana smiled at the memory of the famous hairdresser's words the first time Morey sent her to him. "No, Ruby, I like it like this." Ruby had insisted on being addressed by her first name, because she said being referred to as Mrs. Bailey made her feel old. "The table looks lovely tonight."

"Thank you," Ruby said impatiently as she spied a smear of paint on Rana's sleeve. "You have time to change, dear," she ventured tactfully.

"Does it matter what I'm wearing?"

Ruby sighed with resignation. "I suppose it doesn't. You'd only put on another of your horrid baggy combinations, none of which I'd be caught dead in, and I have about three decades on you. I'm sure, Miss Ramsey, that you could make yourself more attractive if only you'd try." First names didn't apply to her guests.

"I'm not interested in my appearance."

Ruby assessed Rana's flat, functional shoes, her shape-less dress, and the heavy hair hanging on either side of her thin face, a face made to appear even more gaunt by oversized round eyeglasses. Ruby's disapproving expres-sion clearly said, "That's readily apparent." Her actual words were, "Trent's just arrived."

"Yes, I met him upstairs."

Ruby's brown eyes sparkled. "Isn't he the most adorable boy you've ever seen?"

"I didn't expect him to be so . . . young." So young, so good-looking, so virile, and so dangerous to have around, Rana added to herself. What if he recognized her? "I thought you said the new boarder was your cousin."

"Nephew, dear, nephew. He's always been a favorite of mine. My sister spoiled him abominably. Of course I con-stantly chastised her for it. But she couldn't help herself. Who could? He could twist any woman around his little finger. When he called and said he needed a place to stay for the next few weeks, I pretended to be aggravated, but actually I was delighted. He'll be such fun to have around."

"It's only for a few weeks?"

"Yes, and then he'll move back into his house in Houston."

Divorce, no doubt, Rana thought. This nephew of Ruby's, this Trent, needed a place to stay while waiting for a nasty divorce to become final. Well, Aunt Ruby might think he was an "adorable boy," but Rana knew an arrogant, conceited, sexist chauvinist when she saw one. She had every intention of staying out of Mr. Adorable's way. It wouldn't be difficult. A man like Trent Gamblin would never look twice at a woman like "Miss Ramsey."

"Something smells wonderful."

Rana actually jumped at the sound of his cello-mellow voice as he came striding through the portiere that hung across the doorway. His sure footsteps thudded on the hardwood floor. Each strike of his boot heels made the floorboards groan and the china and glass bric-a-brac tinkle against each other.

Ruby was encircled from behind by a pair of brawny brown arms that Michelangelo would have loved to sculpt. Trent bent over her spare body and nuzzled her neck. "Whatcha got cookin', Auntie?"

"Let me go, you big gorilla." She wriggled out of his suffocating embrace, but her cheeks were flushed and her eyes were more animated than usual. "Sit down and behave. Did you wash your hands before coming downstairs?"

"Yes, ma'am," he said meekly, winking slyly at Rana at the same time.

"If you can mind your manners, I'll let you sit at the head of the table. Ask her nicely and Miss Ramsey might pour some sherry for you. Now, excuse me and I'll bring dinner out."

With her electric-blue skirt rustling, Ruby sashayed through the swinging door into the kitchen. When Trent turned around, he was still grinning in approval of his saucy elderly aunt. "She's something, isn't she?" he asked Rana.

"Yes, she is. I like her immensely."

"She's outlived three husbands and one daughter. But none of that got her down." He shook his head in perplexed admiration. "Where do you sit?"

Rana moved toward her accustomed place setting, but he rounded the table with the grace of a *danseur noble* and moved her chair away from the table for her.

Rana was tall. He was much taller. It was odd, and disconcertingly pleasant, to have a man tower over her. Even if she were wearing the highest high heels, Trent Gamblin would be taller than she.

When she was seated in the rosewood lyre-back chair, he took his place at the head of the table. "How long have you lived here?"

"Six months."

"Before that?"

"Back East," she answered obliquely.

He grinned broadly. "I didn't think that was a Texas accent."

She laughed softly. "Hardly." To keep from looking at him, she toyed with her spoon, tracing the elaborate silver pattern with the pad of her middle finger.

"Did you know the other boarder?"

"Guest."

"Huh?"

"Your aunt calls us guests. She says 'boarder' sounds too commercial."

"Ahh." He nodded. His throat was brown and strong. His shirt was opened at the collar, and Rana could see a healthy crop of curling dark hair in the V. Looking at it made her stomach feel weightless, so she averted her eyes. "I'll have to rely on you to acquaint me with the house rules. What time is curfew?"

He was teasing again, and, as before, it annoyed her. She had known plenty of men who played these kinds of flirting games, some of them with more talent than Trent Gamblin. They were games in which a woman was inevitably the prey and a man the hunter. Rana had always resented the masculine assumption that she was interested in such tiresome silliness. She did so now.

Besides, why was this man playing the game with the homely Miss Ramsey?

Then the answer came to her. Except for his aunt, Rana was the only woman around. If there was one aspect of Mr. Gamblin's personality that was readily apparent, it was that he was a born womanizer. Habits were hard to break.

"The former occupant of your apartment was a widow about Ruby's age," Rana explained briskly. "When her health declined, she went to live in Austin, nearer her family."

She took a dainty sip from her water glass, a gesture that she hoped would suspend conversation until their hostess brought in dinner. The dining room seemed awfully close and stuffy this evening. She ruled out the possibility that Trent Gamblin's presence had anything to do with it. Perhaps Ruby needed to adjust the thermostat on the air conditioner.

Disobeying his aunt's instructions to mind his manners, Trent propped his elbow on the table and rested his chin in his hand while he unabashedly studied Miss Ramsey.

Interesting. She couldn't be very old. Either side of thirty by a year or two. She mystified him. Why would a seemingly healthy, intelligent young woman ensconce herself permanently in Aunt Ruby's boardinghouse, quaint and charming though it was? What would motivate a woman to isolate herself deliberately?

Family tragedy, perhaps? A love affair gone awry? Had she been jilted at the altar or something equally shattering?

Miss Ramsey made him think of nothing so much as a spinster schoolmarm of a hundred years ago. Thin face, lank hair—although the candlelight made it shine a color like nothing he'd ever seen before—and that awful gray dress that kept her figure a total secret even from his discerning eyes. She wore no makeup, but her complexion was clear. Unlike that of most redheads, her skin had an olive tint. Actually, though, her hair was too dark just to be called "red." That deep mahogany luster went far beyond merely red.

Her hands, which kept fidgeting with her silverware, were amazingly small and long-fingered, but looked rough.

Her nails had been cut bluntly at the ends of her fingers. She was wearing no polish on them. Nor was she wearing perfume. His nose could detect and name at least fifty different fragrances. Miss Ramsey wasn't wearing one of them. What he hated most were her round eyeglasses. Their blue-tinted lenses hid her eyes completely.

His steady, bold stare was making her nervous. He could tell by the way she kept shifting in her chair. In a mischievous way, he was glad his attention was unsettling her. The poor thing probably needed a thrill or two to enliven her dull, drab existence. If he could oblige, why not? He had nothing better to do.

"Why are you living here, Miss Ramsey?"

"None of your business."

"Ouch! Are you always so prickly?"

"Only when someone is rude enough to stare and ask nosy questions."

"I'm the new kid on the block. You're supposed to be nice to me."

Aunt Ruby's bragging wasn't without some basis. He *was* adorable, particularly when he formed that boyish pout that somehow looked just right on his sensual lips.

"Would you like some sherry?" Rana lifted the lead-crystal decanter.

"Are you serious?" She set it back down. "Got a cold Coors?"

"I don't think Ruby stocks beer."

"I'll bet she's never out of whiskey, though."

Rana's cheeks went red. "I don't—"

"Come on, now, Miss Ramsey. You can tell me. I'm family." He leaned forward conspiratorially, moving his face to within scant inches of hers. "Does the old girl still swizzle her Jack Daniel's?"

Before Rana could form a response, Ruby appeared, pushing a tea cart loaded with silver platters through the kitchen door. "Here we are, dears. I'm sure you're starving, but the rolls needed a few more minutes in the oven."

Trent, still staring at Rana's shocked expression, chuckled softly.

"Trent, stop that irritating sniggering," Ruby scolded. "You always were the rudest child at the table and prone to laugh for no apparent reason. Sit up straight, please, and make yourself useful by carving this roast for me. Miss Ramsey likes hers medium to well done, and be generous with her portion despite her protests. I've managed to put some meat on her meager bones, but she still has a long way to go. Now, isn't this nice?" Ruby said enthusiastically as she took her seat. "This is going to be so cozy, the three of us sharing every meal."

Rana, who was trying to ignore Trent's calculating assessment of just how meager her bones were, was wondering if it would be too obvious if she asked to have her meals in her apartment from now on.

Trent had a hefty appetite. Ruby kept refilling his plate,

until he held up his hands in surrender after eating two and a half portions of everything.

"Please, Aunt Ruby, no more. I'll go to fat."

"Nonsense. You're still a growing boy. I can't send you to summer camp weak and unfit."

Rana choked on a bite of parsleyed potatoes and took a quick drink of water. Her eyes brimmed with tears, but she was careful not to remove her glasses as she blotted them.

"Are you all right, dear?" Ruby asked with concern.

"Fine, fine," Rana choked out. When she was composed, she looked at Trent. "Aren't you a little old to be sent off to summer camp?"

Ruby and Trent both found that highly amusing, and they laughed heartily. "Football summer camp," Ruby explained. "Didn't I tell you that Trent is a professional football player?"

Rana, embarrassed, smoothed her napkin back in her lap. "I don't believe you did."

"He plays with the Houston Mustangs." Ruby beamed proudly, laying her hand on her nephew's muscled arm. "And he's the most important player. The quarterback."

"I see."

"Don't you like football, Miss Ramsey?" Trent inquired. He was a trifle piqued that she hadn't recognized him. Nor had she seemed suitably impressed to discover that she was sharing dinner with a man touted by some sportswriters as the finest quarterback in professional football since Starr and Staubach.

"I don't know very much about it, Mr. Gamblin. But I know more now than I did."

"How's that?"

"I know that the players go to summer camp."

His mouth split into a wide grin. Miss Ramsey had a sense of humor. The next few weeks might not be too taxing after all. In fact, he didn't remember when he'd enjoyed such a relaxing dinner. He didn't have to work at impressing his aunt. She already thought he hung the moon. Any charm he sent in Miss Ramsey's direction was equally certain to be appreciated. No effort was required there either. For the first time in years, he could be himself in the company of females, and it felt good.

"How is your shoulder, Trent?" Ruby turned to Rana to explain. "He has an injury that refuses to heal properly. A shoulder dislocation."

"Separation, Auntie."

"Sorry, a *separation*. His doctor recommended that he get away from his circle of friends and suspend his other activities so his shoulder would have the rest it needs to heal before training camp. Right, dear?"

"Right."

"Is it painful?" Rana asked.

He shrugged. "Sometimes. Only when I overexert myself."

He frowned as he recalled his last appointment with the team doctor. "The damn thing just won't get any better, doc," he had complained. "And you know it's got to be completely well by training camp."

He had gnawed on his lip. If he had another season like the last one, the coach would be scouting for younger and better talent.

Trent wasn't fooling himself. He was thirty-four. His retirement from professional football was imminent. But he wanted one more good—no, *great*—season. He didn't want to retire a broken-down, banged-up failure who caused people to shake their heads sadly and say, "He's lost it, but he just won't admit it." Deep inside him, he knew he hadn't lost it. He wanted to get his shoulder in shape and retire in a blaze of glory. Then he'd go gracefully. Not until then.

"Don't come whining to me, Trent," the doctor had said. "Tom Tandy told me you pulled that shoulder again playing tennis. Tennis, for heaven's sake! Have you lost your mind?"

Trent winced as the doctor's capable hands explored the tender muscles. "I needed to brush up on my ground strokes."

"Bull. I know what kind of strokes you were brushing up on. Tom also told me you were servicing the club's woman pro . . . and I don't mean on the tennis court."

"With tattling friends like Tom—"

"Don't blame this lecture on him. Look, son," the Mustangs' doctor had said, pulling up a stool and speaking to Trent earnestly, "that shoulder is never going to heal if you keep on going the way you have been. Sure, this is the off-season, and you've earned the right to raise a little hell. But training camp is just a few weeks away. Which is more important to you, next football season or the swinging-single's life? Which would you rather be, a Super Bowl quarterback or a superstud?"

Trent had called his aunt that afternoon.

It had been the right decision, he thought now as he leaned back and sipped the coffee Ruby had poured into his china cup. He probably did need the rest, the earlier hours, and regular meals that this sabbatical in Galveston promised. Aunt Ruby certainly wasn't boring. He still had fond memories of his childhood visits with her.

He looked speculatively at the other woman at the table. Miss Ramsey might even prove to be amusing, if she ever lightened up. Maybe he could prod her along.

"What do you do to support yourself?" he asked abruptly.

"Trent! How rude!" his aunt admonished. "Didn't that sister of mine teach you any social graces? You've been around those barbarian teammates of yours too long."

"I want to know." His smile was disarming. "Why beat around the bush? If Miss Ramsey and I are going to be . . . living together, don't you think we should get to know each other?"

His dark eyes had swept down Rana's body, leaving a tide of heat. Rana wished she hadn't felt it. For some unexplainable reason she had been relieved to learn that he wasn't seeking cover from a sticky divorce, though that didn't rule out the possibility that he was married.

She had even felt a twinge of pity for him as an athlete who was obviously worried about his future. She knew enough about the world of professional sports to know that such injuries as shoulder separations could mean the end of a career.

Now, however, when he was looking at her with that familiar "I could eat you for breakfast, little girl" look on his face, her compassion evaporated and her previous aversion returned. With it came her resolution to keep out of his path.

"I paint," she said succinctly.

"Paint? You mean pictures or walls?"

"Neither." She sipped her coffee, creating what she hoped was an irritating delay. "I paint on clothing."

"Clothing?" he asked with a deadpan expression.

"Yes, clothing," she said, staring at him through the blue-tinted lenses of her glasses.

"She's ingenious," Ruby contributed with affected gaiety. She had so hoped her nephew could bring out Miss Ramsey, but during the course of this first meal, her hopes had been dashed. If anything, Miss Ramsey had retreated further into her shell. She seemed to be hiding behind her eyeglasses, shrinking inside her oversized ugly clothing, withdrawing even further behind a veil of secrecy and privacy. "You ought to see some of her creations," Ruby continued, undaunted. "She works too hard at it, though. I'm constantly after her to get out more. To mingle with people her own age."

Trent hadn't taken his eyes off Miss Ramsey. "You do your work here?"

"Yes. I've turned the sitting room of the apartment into a studio. The lighting is good."

"I'm not sure I understand." He stretched his long legs far out in front of him. His knee bumped into hers beneath the table; she quickly pulled hers back. "How do you paint on clothing? What kind of clothing? What do you use?"

She smiled, pleased with his interest in spite of herself. "I buy surplus garments and textiles in warehouses, then hand-paint original designs on them."

He scowled with skepticism. "There's a market for such, uh, clothes?"

"I can afford to pay my rent, Mr. Gamblin," she said tartly. She shoved back her chair abruptly and got to her feet. "It was a wonderful dinner, as usual, Ruby. Good night."

"You're not going to your room so early?" the landlady asked, distressed over Miss Ramsey's sudden mood swing. "I thought we all might have a cup of tea in the parlor."

"Excuse me tonight. I'm tired. Mr. Gamblin." She gave him a cool nod before stalking from the dining room.

"Well I'll be damned," Trent muttered. "What bee got up her—"

"Trent, don't be crude!" Ruby interrupted. "Wait! What are you— Where—"

Heedless of his aunt's surprised sputtering, he stood, tossed down his napkin, and left the table with the same angry urgency Miss Ramsey had displayed only seconds before. His long legs covered ground faster than she could. He caught up with her just as she reached the stairs. "Miss Ramsey!"

His voice carried with it the imperiousness of a drill sergeant. She stopped with her foot poised on the second step and turned around.

Before she could prevent it, he had her right hand firmly enfolded in his. "You didn't give me a chance to tell you how glad I am to find myself in your delightful company." Regardless of his seething anger, he spoke in dulcet tones. *No* woman walked out on Trent Gamblin. "*Enchanted,* Miss Ramsey." Lifting her hand, he pressed his mouth to the back of it.

She tried to hold in her gasp but failed. She felt as if she had been punched in the middle. Aftershocks rippled through her. Snatching her hand away from his, she spoke a frosty good night and haughtily retreated upstairs.

Trent was still smiling when he returned to the dining room. "I don't like the gloating expression on your face, Trent," Ruby said sternly.

He resumed his seat and poured himself another cup of coffee from the silver pot. "Miss Ramsey might act like a prickly old maid, but she's still a woman."

"I hope that you won't do anything indiscreet or treat Miss Ramsey with anything but the utmost respect. She is a dear girl, but treasures her privacy. In all these months, she hasn't divulged any personal information about herself. My guess is that there's a great sadness in her history. Please don't provoke her."

"I wouldn't think of it," he said with a smile that was anything but sincere.

Since his aunt had always adored him, she didn't question his earnestness. "Good. Now, be a sweetheart and come into the kitchen with me while I clean up. I want to hear everything that's been going on in your life."

"Even the raunchy stuff?"

She giggled and squeezed his chin between her fingers. "I want to hear the raunchy stuff first."

Trent followed his aunt into her kitchen, but his mind was still on Miss Ramsey. What the hell was her first name, anyway? He had noticed, in spite of her clothes—clothes that a bag lady would be ashamed to wear—that she had a remarkably graceful, fluid walk. Her posture was proud. The hand he had so arrogantly kissed might have been un-manicured, but it was dainty to the point of fragility. For some reason, despite the rough skin and the faint smell of paint and turpentine, he had enjoyed kissing it very much.

* * *

Upstairs in the bedroom of her apartment, which took up the east side of the second story, Rana undressed. She had avoided mirrors in the last six months, but she looked at herself carefully now. The cheval glass stood in one corner of the antique-furnished room, so she could see her whole image reflected.

She had left New York weighing one hundred and ten pounds. Stretched over her five-foot-nine-inch frame, the flesh had been thinly distributed. Thanks to Ruby's culinary arts, not to mention her nagging, Rana had gained almost twenty pounds. By any other standards, she was still thin. To herself, she looked fat. Her hipbones no longer protruded from a concave abdomen. Her breasts had become rounder, softer, far more feminine.

The extra poundage was also evident in her face. The cheekbones made legendary by photographs published in the world's leading fashion magazines didn't seem so pronounced, now that the cheeks beneath them had filled out.

She took off the unnecessary eyeglasses. Those topaz-green eyes that had lured hundreds of thousands of women into buying eye-shadow collections with names such as Sahara Sands and Forest Gems stared back at her. Artfully made up, they were spectacular. Even without makeup, their slanting almond shape was distinctive and arresting. Too arresting not to be camouflaged by tinted glasses if she wanted her identity to remain a secret.

She forced her lips into a smile. Her teeth were going crooked again. Her mother would fly into a tizzy if she could see them. How much money had Susan Ramsey spent straightening Rana's teeth? Yet without the retainer Rana had been advised to sleep in every night of her life, her four front teeth were stubbornly overlapping again.

Picking up a hairbrush, she swept back the heavy strands hanging on either side of her face. She shook her head, as she had been taught to do. There it was, the Rana Look. A mane of dark red hair framing an exotic face. A blurred, diluted version, true, but a glimpse that brought back painful memories.

Even now she could feel the agent's tobacco-stained fingers pinching her chin as they jerked Rana's head this way and that to capture certain angles. "She's just too . . . too *exotic*-looking, Mrs. Ramsey. She's lovely, but . . . foreign. Yes, that's it. She's not all-American enough."

"You've already got all-American models," Susan Ramsey said with disgust. "My Rana's different. That's what makes her an undiscovered treasure."

No one, not the appraising agent, not the yawning photographer, least of all her mother, noticed Rana wince. She was hungry. A cheeseburger came to mind, and the thought made her mouth water. No sense in torturing herself. She would be lucky to be allowed low-calorie dressing on her lettuce salad if she got lunch at all.

"I'm sorry," the agent said, gathering the glossy eight-by-ten pictures of Rana into a messy stack and handing them back to Susan Ramsey. "She's a beautiful girl; she's just not for us. Have you tried Ford? Eileen did very well with Ali McGraw, and she had dark hair and eyes."

Stuffing the pictures back into a large portfolio and roughly taking Rana by the arm, Susan had marched out of the office. In the elevator, she marked that agent's name off her long list. "Don't worry, Rana. Everyone in New York can't be that blindly stupid. Please stand up straight. And next time will you please try smiling a little more?"

"I'm slouching because I'm weak with hunger, Mother. I had one slice of melba toast and a half a grapefruit for breakfast. We've walked miles. My feet hurt. Can't we stop somewhere, sit down, and eat?"

"Just a few more interviews," Susan said absently as she scanned the remaining names on her list.

"But I'm tired."

Susan ushered Rana out of the elevator when it reached the lobby floor. "You truly are selfish and self-centered, Rana. I got you out of that unfortunate marriage. I sold my home to get the money to bring you to New York. I'm sacrificing my own life for your career. And this is the thanks I get. All you do is whine."

Rana didn't say what she was thinking, that the modeling career had been her mother's idea, not her own, that it had been Susan's desire to sell their house in Des Moines and move to New York, and that the marriage had been unfortunate because of Susan's constant meddling.

"Our next appointment is in fifteen minutes. If you stop dawdling, we'll be there five minutes early. That'll give you time to repair your makeup. Please remember to smile. You never know when a smile or a sexy glance will pay off. One of these agents is bound to see your potential."

The agent who finally did was Morey Fletcher. His office wasn't at a prestigious address. He was overweight, gruff, disheveled, balding. His name was far down on Susan's list. But he looked past the mother and saw the nineteen-year-old girl hovering in the background. His stomach did somersaults, and it wasn't because of the corned-beef sandwich he had had sent up from the deli downstairs. If a jaded professional like himself could be moved by that face and those eyes, he reasoned that John Q. Public would be too.

"Sit down, Miss Ramsey." He offered a chair to the girl first. Surprised, she collapsed in it and immediately slipped off her shoes. He smiled, and she smiled back.

Within two days a contract had been drawn up, repeatedly examined by Susan, and eventually signed. That was the beginning.

Just thinking about the months that followed made Rana weary. Her shoulders slumped. Her head dropped forward and her hair swung down to hide the classic cheekbones again.

She pulled on a ragged T-shirt to sleep in and padded to the window. If she listened closely she could hear the incessant waves of the Gulf of Mexico rolling toward the shore a few blocks away. Cicadas and crickets made their shrill racket in the thick branches of the trees. The novelty of these sounds still intrigued her. They were so different from the city sounds that had filtered up to the thirty-second-story window of her Upper East Side apartment. She much preferred this quaintly furnished bedroom to the stark modernity of her professionally decorated apartment in New York. The peacefulness of it was something she would always treasure.

Except that tonight, she wasn't so peaceful.

She discovered her restlessness as soon as she slipped between the sheets. Her mind kept returning to the man who now lived across the hall from her. He so fit the stereotype of the macho man that he was laughable. Strange, though, she mused, she didn't feel like laughing.

She was relieved on one account—he hadn't recognized her. Of course his reading material probably ran more toward *Sports Illustrated* than it did to *Vogue*. Miss Ramsey hardly looked like the model in the cosmetics commercials on television. And no one would expect the elusive Rana to turn up in a boardinghouse in Galveston, Texas.

He had his nerve, kissing her hand that way. He'd done it out of sheer spite. How was she going to stand living under the same roof with a man who had such an inflated ego?

She would ignore him, she decided.

But she was already listening for his tread on the stairs and wondering what he was doing. Aggravated with herself, she punched her pillow and erased Trent Gamblin from her thoughts. But as she drifted to sleep, she was thinking about his smile and how attractively it rearranged his entire face.

And on the back of her hand lingered the burning sensation left by his lips.

Two

She almost stepped on him when she pulled open the door to her apartment late the next morning. He was stretched out on the floor of the hallway doing push-ups.

"Oh!" She flattened her hand against her leaping heart.

He bounced up. "Good morning."

Her first impulse was to scurry back into the safety of her apartment and slam the door, shielding herself from the temptation to feast her eyes on his nakedness.

For all practical purposes he *was* naked. Only a pair of brief nylon running shorts stood between him and indecency. They, however, tested the perimeters of what could be considered decent. The elastic waistband rode well below his waist . . . well below his navel, in fact. Soaked with perspiration, the trunks clung to his skin as though they had been plastered to his body.

As to the size and shape of . . . everything . . . he now had no secrets from her. He was ample and perfect.

Rana felt her throat closing after the hasty glance downward her eyes took, despite her instructions for them to stay well above his waist.

"Good morning," she said with a wheeze. She told herself to look anywhere but at him.

His running shoes and a damp, limp pair of athletic socks had been piled in the doorway of his apartment. Through the open door, she could see that the room was a mess. Clothing as yet unpacked spilled out of suitcases. Boxes were stacked on top of each other.

"You've been exercising?" she asked for lack of anything else to say.

"Yeah, running on the beach. It was great."

He was sweaty. Quarts of liquid must have poured out of that impressive masculine body. Droplets of perspiration beaded on his skin and collected strands of dark, curly chest hair into sodden clumps. It trickled through a silky strip of ebony hair that halved his midriff and arrowed down toward his navel. He raised his forearm to wipe the moisture off his brow. Looking into the shadowy hollow of his armpit was like committing an intimate act with him. Rana averted her eyes guiltily.

"Is your . . . Does your shoulder . . . I mean, are push-ups good for your shoulder?" Her own palms were perspiring. She tried as unobtrusively as possible to blot them against her baggy gray gabardine pants.

"They don't hurt it. Different muscles."

"I see."

"You do?"

"Well, I mean, push-ups are for arms and . . . and chest, aren't they?"

"Yeah," he said. "The pecs. Do you ever work out?"

"Not my . . . my . . . uh, pecs." His mouth fashioned a wide grin. "I jog sometimes," she rushed to say.

"Why don't you jog with me tomorrow?"

"I don't think so," she said, edging around him. "Well, 'bye."

"Pardon me for using the hallway, but I didn't have room in my apartment. I haven't unpacked yet."

"I was on my way down to the kitchen. Excuse me."

When she was beside him, he said, "Miss Ramsey?"

"Hm?" Politely, albeit unwisely, she turned to face him. They were now close enough for her to catch the tangy, salty, sea-scented fragrance he had carried in from the beach. It wasn't at all unpleasant.

"Do you know how push-ups should really be done?"

"I've never . . . no, I don't."

"To really maximize benefits of the exercise, it's best to do push-ups with someone lying on your back."

She swallowed. "Lying on your back?"

He leaned against the wall and crossed his arms over his chest. She wished he hadn't, because that casual stance only served to make the hard muscles of his chest bulge. He was cooling off; his nipples were erect. Again Rana felt that she had seen something forbidden and lowered her eyes. A foolhardy decision as it turned out. His bare ankles were crossed, too, and something else bulged between his thighs.

"Yeah. Someone to add weight."

"To make the muscles work harder?" she guessed.

"That's the idea. Now, I was thinking, I don't suppose *you* . . ." He cocked his head to one side and let his incomplete suggestion dangle while his brown eyes twinkled with a thousand devilish lights. "No, I guess not," he finished briskly. "Never mind."

Her cheeks were suffused with vivid color. At first the blush was caused by embarrassment, then by anger, as she saw an insinuating smile break across his sensual mouth.

"As I said, I was on my way to the kitchen." She turned her back on him and hurried away.

Arrogant idiot! she fumed to herself when she heard his chuckle following her down the stairs. What did it matter to her if he wanted to run around as naked as a savage and sweat like a pig? She scoffed at him, but her hands were trembling as she took a glass from the cabinet and poured a soda over ice.

Rather than return to her apartment, where she might risk meeting him again, she sat down at the small table in Ruby's homey kitchen. Taking up the pad and pencil always left beneath the telephone, Rana idly sketched out some ideas she'd been toying with. Birds of paradise painted over a wash of pale lavender? A scarlet hibiscus filling the entire back of a bodice? Or how about a bold abstract design with orange and black and turquoise?

"Brainstorming?"

She dropped the pencil clumsily and, in her attempt to retrieve it, almost knocked over her glass of soda. "I wish you wouldn't sneak up on me like that," she told Trent crossly.

"Sorry. I thought you heard me. Guess you were lost in thought."

She directed an accusing stare down at his bare feet. "If you would wear shoes, maybe I could hear you."

"I rubbed a blister on my little toe this morning. Hurts like hell."

If he was expecting sympathy, he was in for a disappointment.

She wanted to ask why he found it necessary to run around half dressed, but she lacked the nerve. Besides, she didn't want him to know that she had noticed his cutoffs. The denim shorts gloved his thighs, hips, and manhood with a heart-stopping, breath-suspending fit. He now wore a sleeveless Houston Mustangs T-shirt that had been cut off just below his breast, leaving his midriff bare. His torso was so squarely symmetrical it could have been mathematically designed with a ruler. Her eyes were involuntarily drawn to his navel. Could navels be considered beautiful? Or was his merely mysterious in a sexy way? In either case, she wanted to investigate it.

"Is Auntie around?"

Rana yanked her eyes, attention, and imagination away from his lower abdomen and gestured toward a note secured to the refrigerator by a magnet shaped like a head of cabbage. "She went out for a while."

"Hm." His brow wrinkled. "She said she had stocked some fruit juice for me. Any idea where?"

"Check the refrigerator."

He opened the door and surveyed the contents. "Milk, a bottle of Chablis, diet sodas," he said, giving her a glance over his shoulder, "and something in a little brown crock marked by masking tape with 'Do not throw out' written on it."

"That's bacon grease."

"I don't think that'll quench my thirst."

Realizing her private interlude had come to an end the moment he entered the kitchen, she got out of her chair and, with a long-suffering sigh she made certain he heard, said, "Sometimes she keeps extra supplies on the sleeping porch." She went through the doorway leading to the screened back porch.

"Believe it or not, I've actually slept out here," he said.

"Really?"

"Lots of summer nights when I was a kid and my mom and I would come visiting."

She feigned disinterest, though the picture of a tough little boy with dark hair and skinned knees came to her mind. "What about your father?"

"He was killed in an airplane crash overseas before I

was old enough to remember him. Mom never remarried. She died two years ago."

He was as alone in the world as she, but she couldn't let herself feel sympathy for him. She couldn't let herself feel *anything* for him, especially now that the scent of the beach had been replaced by that of clean skin, shaving soap, and citrus cologne.

She checked the pantry, where Ruby stored everything from toilet tissue and dishwashing soap to homemade jam. On one shelf Rana found a variety of canned fruit juices. "Apple, grapefruit, or orange?"

"Orange."

He filled up the doorway between her and the kitchen. His legs were long and lean, but as hard as tree trunks. His biceps were lined with blue veins that her eyes followed all the way down his tanned forearms to the backs of his hands. A surgical scar was visible around his right elbow. Two of the fingers on his right hand were crooked from having been broken. Battle scars of his profession, she supposed.

"Excuse me," she mumbled when she reached the door. He moved aside to let her pass, and she carried the can of orange juice into the kitchen. "Watch me so you'll know where everything is next time."

"You have my undivided attention, Miss Ramsey."

Ignoring his teasing inflection, she opened the can with the opener she had located in a drawer and repeated the motions she'd gone through only minutes before in preparing her own drink. "There." She handed the glass to him.

"Thanks." He winked at her. Raising the glass to his lips and tilting his head back, he drank every drop of the juice. Rana watched his Adam's apple slide up and down only three times as he drained the glass.

"More, please." He extended the glass to her, and, dumbfounded that he could consume so much so quickly, she refilled it automatically. He gulped that glassful down the same way, smacking his lips with satisfaction when he was done. "Ahh. Now, this glass, I can drink more slowly."

"You mean you want more?" she asked incredulously as he motioned to her to fill the glass again.

His eyes seemed to want to bore through her eyeglasses. "That's only one of the unquenchable thirsts I have, Miss Ramsey." Then his gaze slid down to her mouth.

"Hello, Ruby!"

Rana jumped as if she'd been shot. She recognized the postman's cheerful voice. It was his custom to visit with Ruby every day when he delivered the mail. Had Ruby been twenty years younger, Rana would have said they were flirting. Perhaps that was exactly what it was, despite Ruby's age.

She set the can of juice on the countertop. "Serve yourself from now on, Mr. Gamblin. In here, Mr. Felton," she called out to the postman, hurrying to the back porch. "Ruby's not here. Mercy, we have quite a lot today, don't we?"

"Bills, mostly. A few magazines. Got everything? Tell Ruby I said hello."

"I will."

Rana returned to the kitchen with the mail and dumped it on the table. As she sorted through it, checking to see if anything was addressed to her, Trent moved up behind her.

It had almost become second nature to him to study and analyze Miss Ramsey. She was so different from the women he knew. He'd never seen uglier clothes than the ones she was wearing today. Her slacks, which she had gathered at the waist with a wide, functional leather belt, would have fit a woman twice her size. And they would have been right at home on a battleship. They were that drab, that utilitarian, that ugly.

If she had a fanny, he couldn't begin to guess its proportions. The shape of her legs, too, remained a mystery. Goodwill would have rejected the paint-splattered man's shirt she was wearing. The sleeves had been rolled back to reveal her forearms, but the shapeless vest she wore over the shirt hung straight to her hips. She couldn't have much bosom, but in spite of himself he was curious to know just how much. He was almost crazy with curiosity about her breasts.

He stared down at the center part of her hair. She hadn't gone to any trouble to style it. It hung heavy and straight down her back, well brushed, but otherwise uncared for. It sure as hell smelled good, though. He liked the floral fragrance of her shampoo. Or was that bubble bath he smelled?

The thought of Miss Ramsey languishing in a bubble bath was ludicrous. But all women, no matter how homely, enjoyed feminine indulgences like that, didn't they? he wondered. Sure, she took bubble baths. Of course she did.

And what did she put on afterward? Scanty, lacy underthings that were as delicate as spider webs? Somehow he couldn't picture her in anything frivolous or fantasy-inspiring. She probably wore opaque cotton that covered and contained completely.

Why the hell was he wondering about her lingerie anyway? Was he actually standing here speculating on Miss Ramsey's underthings? Dear Lord, maybe he needed a woman worse than he'd thought. Maybe his body was desperately sex-starved and just hadn't telegraphed the message to his brain yet. Maybe he should call Tom and have him send some willing woman to him. Without delay. Federal Express.

No, no, he thought, rejecting the idea almost immediately. Hell. That was why he'd left Houston, wasn't it? To get away from all that carousing? He'd been partying too hard. The closest he'd get to a woman for the next few weeks was through his fantasies. And Miss Ramsey was the only one around who was near his age. His choices were limited, so why not let a few fantasies about her play around in his mind? They were harmless.

He had no doubt that she was feminine to some extent,

even if she was no more approachable than a barbed-wire fence. Confusion had been written all over her face when she'd stepped into the hallway and accidentally encountered him doing his calisthenics.

He *could* have made room to do the push-ups in his own apartment, but he had perversely hoped she might stumble across him in the hallway. The poor dear had probably never seen a man that close to naked before. Did she know what male sweat looked and smelled like? Probably not until this morning. Certainly she had seemed flustered. Trent had to suppress a chuckle even now at the memory of her shocked face. But she had liked what she saw. He'd stake his reputation as a Casanova on that.

"Anything for me?"

His breath struck the top of her head. Only then did Rana realize how close to her he was standing. "No," she said, hurriedly sorting through the rest of the envelopes. She tossed the mail back down on the table. When she did, the cover of one of Ruby's fashion magazines fell open.

Rana gasped.

There she was, svelte and sexy, reclining on a white sheet. Her mahogany hair was spread like a fan behind her head. It had taken the hairdresser and photographer a full hour to get it just right. Her cheekbones stood out prominently, and above them her eyes were sultry. Her lips glistened, sulky and suggestive, in a half smile.

She was wearing her trademark white. That was Morey's

stipulation; he would agree to let her do the underwear ad only if it was met. "Rana only wears white, you know," he had told the advertising men. They had wanted her, and they had been willing to meet any condition and pay the exorbitant price she demanded.

In the ad, one of her knees was provocatively raised. She had had a bruise on her thigh from banging it on a taxi door the day before. It had been a challenge for the makeup artist to cover it up, but eventually he'd made her skin look like it had been polished with oil, then buffed. Looking at the photograph, one could almost feel the silky texture of her olive skin.

The bikini panties she wore sliced well below her prominent hipbones. In the photograph her tank top was being pushed up to the undercurve of her breast by a man's hand. The man, lying beside her but out of the camera's range, had had a face like a potato, but the hands of a poet. He made his living doing everything from patting babies' behinds in disposable-diaper commercials to opening cans of beer so they would foam over the top.

The ad was captioned, "Softness has never felt this soft."

It had been chilly in the studio. Her nipples had contracted and were plainly defined against the cotton-knit tank top. The ad-agency rep had been ecstatic over the effect. His client had asked for sex without lewdness. The photographer was interested only in the focus and lighting. His assistant joked that the hand model was taking secret gropes of Rana's breast while no one was looking. Susan Ramsey took offense and began to virulently protest his "lecherous" humor. Since the assistant was also the photographer's lover, *he* took offense at her name-calling and threatened to have her evicted from the studio if she didn't shut up.

Through it all Rana had lain there, bored, tired, her back aching from holding the pose so long and her stomach growling from perpetual hunger.

"Nice."

The deep male voice rumbled close to her ear, bringing her back into the present. She slapped the magazine cover closed.

"What's the matter? Didn't you like it?" Trent asked, obviously amused by her prudish reaction to the erotic ad.

"Yes . . . no . . . I—I've got to get back to work."

She shoved her way past him and virtually ran up the stairs. After shutting herself in her apartment, she slumped against the door, gulping for breath, expectantly waiting for him to come chasing after her, waving the magazine, his mouth agape now that he recognized her.

Then she realized that her fear of discovery was ridiculous. Neither Trent nor anyone else would recognize her from that ad. Miss Ramsey matched the woman in the picture about as much as the hand model's face matched his beautiful hands. There was no apparent connection between the two.

Eventually she pushed herself away from the door and

went back to work on the wrap skirt she'd been painting when she'd decided to take a break. It seemed like centuries ago.

She had had two shocks. First, seeing Trent Gamblin during his workout, and then seeing herself in that magazine. For six months she had lived her reclusive life without any real threat of discovery. Even when she had notified Morey and her mother of her new address, she had warned them that if they badgered her into returning to New York, she would disappear again and never let them know where she was.

Now, with Trent living in the house, detection suddenly seemed imminent. Her private sphere had been invaded. Ruby's vanity prevented her from wearing eyeglasses, even though her vision wasn't too keen. So despite the fact that she read her fashion magazines faithfully, she had never connected her dowdy boarder with the dazzling Rana.

Would her nephew be more astute?

Rana's contemplation of her problem was interrupted by the ringing of the telephone. Out of habit, she wiped her hands with a cloth before answering her extension.

"Hi, Barry," she said happily when the caller identified himself.

"I hope you're hard at work. You're in demand."

"I am?" She was pleased; their arrangement was proving to be as lucrative for him as it was for her. Rana had met Barry Golden in New York, where he worked as a fashion coordinator for a major department store. He loved the fashion industry, but hated the city. When he'd come into a small fortune left to him by his grandfather, he had returned to his hometown of Houston and opened an exquisite store that catered to wealthy socialites.

He had told Rana when he left New York that if she ever needed anything, she should let him know. She had taken him up on that offer six months ago. If it was blind luck that had brought her to the Galveston boardinghouse, it was Barry who had brought her to the Houston area originally.

Her idea of hand-painting articles of clothing had captured his imagination, and he had enthusiastically agreed to put some of her designs in his store on consignment. They had sold immediately, and his clientele began clamoring for more. She now worked almost solely on commission.

"Your designs are the hottest thing since tamales," Barry told her.

Smiling, she could just imagine him drawing deeply on one of the thin black cigarettes he chain-smoked. He was irascible, brutally frank, and often downright rude. But his rudeness was in direct proportion to his affection for the person to whom he directed it. The more outrageous he was, the better his customers liked him.

Beneath Barry's abrasive veneer, Rana had detected a caring human being whose affectations were a defense mechanism. She thought he was probably fulfilling everyone's expectations of him, just as she had done until six months ago.

"Was Mrs. Tupplewhite happy with her hostess gown?"

"My darling, when she saw it, she almost burst the seams of this really tacky dress she was wearing. It was the most hideous plaid I've ever seen."

"Did you sell it to her?"

"But of course." He cackled. "Some of my customers may have no taste, but I'm not stupid."

"Is that why you agreed to feature my designs in your store?"

"You are an exception to every rule I know, love. You were the first model I'd ever met who wasn't obsessed by her own image in the mirror. You were a doll to work with during those fashion shows I organized. You weren't pushy."

"My mother did all the pushing for me."

"Don't get me started on *her*, or I'll keep you all day. Suffice it to say that I adore you and your work. I feel almost guilty about selling these works of art commercially."

"I'll bet," Rana said drolly.

He sighed theatrically. "Ahh, my, you know me too well. Now, enough of this," he said, switching moods abruptly. "When are you coming into Houston? When will the wrap skirt be finished for Mrs. Rutherford? She's making a nuisance of herself, calling three times a day."

"By the end of the week."

"Good. I've got four more orders for you."

"Four?"

"Yes, four, and I've raised your price."

"Barry! Again? I'm not doing this for money. I can still support myself on my residuals."

"Don't be ridiculous. In our society we do everything for money. And these rich broads don't quibble about price. The more something costs their husbands, the better they like it. Now, be a good child and shut up about the price tags I place on your designs. Are you still holding to that ridiculous rule that you refuse to meet with the customers personally?"

"Yes."

"For the same reason?"

"Yes. There's an outside chance one of them might recognize me."

"So what? I'd be delighted. You know how I feel about that absurd disguise."

"I'm happier than I've been in years, Barry," she said softly.

"Very well. I won't nag. But I do have something different and exciting to discuss with you when I see you."

"What is it?"

"Never mind now. Just go back to work on Mrs. Rutherford's skirt."

"Okay. I'll—Hold on a sec. Ruby's at my door." Rana laid down the receiver and scrambled to the door. But it wasn't Ruby who stood on the threshold. It was Trent. He was leaning lazily against the jamb.

"Got a Band-Aid?"

"I'm on the phone," she replied shortly. He looked positively mouth-watering, and she was irritated with herself for noticing.

"I don't mind waiting."

He pushed past her, so she had no choice but to let him come in. She certainly couldn't remove him physically from her apartment. Giving him a dirty look, she went back to the telephone.

"Barry, I'm sorry. I've got to go."

"So do I. I'll see you later in the week, love."

"Yes, Friday. Good-bye."

"Who's Barry?" Trent asked baldly the moment she hung up the phone.

"None of your business. What was it you wanted?"

"A boyfriend?"

She stared at him angrily through the tinted lenses of her glasses and mentally counted to ten. "Yes, Barry is a man and yes, he's a friend, but no, he's not a boyfriend in the way you suggest. It was a Band-Aid you interrupted me for, wasn't it?"

"Are you sure he's not a boyfriend? Aren't you seeing him on Friday? Sounds like a date to me."

"Do you want a Band-Aid or not?"

She tossed her hair back angrily, and belligerently planted her fists on her hips. Trent was delighted to see the soft, round evidence of breasts beneath her shabby shirt. Nice breasts. Very nice breasts. He smiled. "Please."

She went into her bathroom and found a tin of Band-Aids in the medicine cabinet over her sink. She fumbled with the lid, finally got the thing open, took out one of the bandages, and pivoted on her heel. Trent was standing behind her. She ran right into him.

It all happened in a moment's time, but it seemed to Rana that it lasted forever.

Automatically her hands came up and flattened against the wall of his chest. His hands clasped her upper arms in an effort to steady her. For a split second, their bodies touched. Everywhere. Chests, tummies, thighs, and everything in between came together with a soft, solid impact that had drastic repercussions.

Electrical circuits connected. Heat was generated. Invisible sparks flew.

Rana ground the heels of her hands against his chest to push herself away from him. He, too, fell back a step. He felt as dazed as he'd been the last time Mean Joe Greene slammed into him behind the line of scrimmage.

Two sets of lungs were suddenly starved for air, and the only sound in the room was their struggle for oxygen.

"Here's . . . here's the Band-Aid." A tremulous hand extended the bandage toward him.

He took it. "Thanks." Yes, she definitely had breasts. And firm thighs.

He turned away, and she breathed a vast sigh of relief. But he didn't head for the door. Instead, he sat down on the edge of her sofa and propped one foot over the opposite knee. He grappled with the stubborn cellophane wrapper and after a few seconds gave up. "Can you open this for me, please?"

"Certainly." She lunged forward to take the Band-Aid from him once again. She just wanted him to go quickly. To leave her hermit's cave. This was her refuge, her safety, and he was an unwanted intruder. "I'm sure Ruby has some Band-Aids," she said, hoping he would hear the unspoken reprimand in her voice.

"I'm sure she does, too, but she still isn't home. I'm sorry if I'm disturbing you."

He was disturbing her, all right. She hadn't been involved with a man since her marriage, seven years ago. Men were off-limits. Men were unnecessary risks. Friends like Barry and Morey were fine. Business associates were fine as long as they kept to business. But never, *never* would she allow herself to love a man again. That was her creed. She had sworn never to get so sexually stirred up that her hand trembled as it was trembling now. One disaster was enough. "I have work to do, and I'm not getting much done today." And you are the reason, she added silently.

Frowning slightly, he took the bandage from her and carefully wrapped it around his little toe. "There. That should keep it from getting any worse." He stood up. "You do good work, Ana."

"What?" What had he called her? He had even pronounced it with a soft "a," to rhyme with her real name.

"I noticed as soon as I came in. Very interesting."

He motioned his head toward her work area, where garments in various stages of completion were spread out. He walked toward them and studied her current project, Mrs. Rutherford's skirt. It sported a cluster of tiger lilies extending from the hem to the waistband on the left side. And there, crawling up one spotted petal, was her discreet cursive signature, "Ana R." She and Barry had agreed on the backward spelling of her name as a trademark.

"My dear, it will add to the value of the garments if they're signed. All original works of art *must* be signed," Barry had said. Labeling them with "Rana" would have been like having a banner headline in the *Houston Chronicle* announcing where she was.

"I've been wondering what your first name is," Trent said.

He had very good eyes to have spotted that name. Naturally, he assumed that the capital "r" stood for Ramsey. This nephew of Ruby's was no cerebral slouch. Rana must be very careful. At least she had leased the apartment under that name as well, so there would be no discrepancy should he and Ruby start comparing notes.

When he turned to face her again, it took a tremendous amount of willpower on her part not to flinch. "It's a very pretty name," he said.

"Thank you." Was he trying to see behind her glasses? His eyes seemed unusually perceptive and probing. They wandered toward her mouth again, and, as before, she felt light-headed. "If you'll excuse me, Mr. Gamblin—"

"Call me Trent now. I intend to call you Ana. After all, we're neighbors." His smile was slanted, a little higher on the right side, and entirely too appealing. Or maybe his appeal was due to the way his hair fell boyishly over his forehead.

"As I was saying, Mr. Gamblin"—she stressed his last name—"I'm busy."

"You know what they say about all work and no play." He hitched his thumbs into the belt loops of his cutoffs. "I was thinking about taking in a matinee this afternoon. Why don't you come along?"

Her mouth fell open. "I can't go to—"

"Clint Eastwood. You think he's sexy, don't you?"

"Yes, he is, but I—"

"I'll buy the popcorn."

"No—"

"Double butter. I like it real buttery, don't you?"

"Yes, but—"

"Do you mind if I lick my fingers?"

"No, I—"

"Good. If you say please, I'll lick yours too."

"Mr. Gamblin!" she cried in a desperate attempt to stop his flow of flirtatious chatter. She drew in a deep breath. "You may be idle and have the time to joke the day away, but I'm busy. Will you please leave?"

His smile collapsed, his easygoing posture became rigid, and his lips drew into a thin line of vexation. "Well, pardon me. I won't keep you from your work a moment longer."

He stamped toward the door, and nearly tore it from its hinges when he opened it. "Thanks again for the Band-Aid," he said over his shoulder before he slammed the door behind him.

"Uptight biddy," he muttered as he made his way into his own apartment, which still looked as if a hurricane had been through it. "Prissy, prickly, prudish." He slammed his door behind him, hoping the reverberation overturned one of her paint bottles. "Who needs you, lady?"

Just who did she think she was, ordering him around as if he were an ill-behaved child? No woman had ever had the gall to speak to him like that. *He* chose the time he left a woman's company, not the other way around.

"Mr. Gamblin, Mr. Gamblin," he repeated in a nasty, mocking voice.

Damn! As if the next few weeks of exile weren't going to be punishment enough, he was living across the hall from a nun!

"Bet she nearly fainted when I mentioned licking her fingers. Bet she—"

That was it! he realized. She was a plain woman. There had been little or no excitement in her sorrowful existence, especially of a sexual nature. No doubt there was a giant void in the romance department of her life. In walked a man. "Reasonably good-looking," he mumbled immodestly. She didn't know how to act, so she was putting up barriers.

Sure. Why hadn't he seen it before? She wouldn't be so defensive if he left her cold, would she?

A gleam sparkled in his eyes as he formulated a plan that would tear down her defenses. It would be fun. It would be a challenge. It would be something to occupy his mind while he was here. He couldn't study his playbook all the time.

He didn't consider the real reason he wanted to pursue her. For just a moment, when her slight body had come in contact with his, he had responded with heat and hardness. Unthinkable as it was, he, the prince of singles bars and boudoirs, had been fully aroused by Miss Ana Ramsey.

Three

I'm going to treat you ladies to a movie tonight."

Trent made the announcement as Ruby was ladling raspberry sauce over the cheesecake. "A movie! You dear boy, what fun!"

"I thought it would be," Trent said. "Clint Eastwood."

"Oooh," Ruby said. "He's so sexy, he makes me shiver."

"Better take an I.D. along, Auntie. It's rated 'R,' and they might not let you in."

"Oh, you!"

Trent leaned back in his chair and flashed his aunt a huge smile. But he kept a surreptitious eye on Ana Ramsey. Just as he'd expected, her cheeks were turning red with anger.

"Thank you just the same, Mr. Gamblin, but you'll have to excuse me," she said tightly.

"You're not going?" Ruby asked, evidently aghast. "How

could you turn down an invitation to go to a Clint Eastwood movie?"

"I have work to do. I didn't get much accomplished today." Rana shot Trent a fulminating look, which he missed, because he had devoted himself entirely to eating his cheesecake.

"But you never work in the evenings," Ruby argued. "You told me that you didn't have enough light to work at night."

"Well, that's true," Rana said, "but tonight is an exception."

"Aw come on, Ana, be a sport," Trent drawled. "You'll mess up my plans if you don't come with us." He reached into the breast pocket of his shirt, took out three theater tickets, and waved them at her. "I've already bought your ticket."

"He's already bought your ticket," Ruby echoed.

"I'm sorry," Rana said ungraciously. "He shouldn't have taken that liberty until I had consented to go. He'll just have to return it and get his money back."

Trent squinted down at the small print on the ticket and read aloud, "No cash refunds." He shrugged apologetically. "See? It says so right here." He extended the ticket toward her. "No cash refunds."

"No cash refunds, Miss Ramsey," Ruby said plaintively. She was glad that Trent had been thoughtful enough to include Miss Ramsey in their evening. The younger woman had no friends, as far as Ruby knew, except for someone named Barry, who owned the store in Houston where she sold her things. Ruby could count on one hand the times Miss Ramsey had gone out for an evening. If anyone could stand a night at the movies, it was she.

Rana, unaware of Ruby's musings, glared at Trent. He had put her on the spot deliberately. Well, she would turn the tables on him. "I thought you said you were going to a matinee." Nonchalantly, he took a sip of coffee before answering her. "I changed my mind. Movies are more fun when they're shared. Not to mention popcorn." He winked to remind her of their earlier conversation about popcorn. Rana fumed.

Ruby sprang to her feet with the impetus of a Jack-in-the-box. "Then it's all settled. I'll—"

"I haven't agreed to go."

"But you will, won't you, dear?" Ruby's smile was so pathetic, so pleading, that Rana couldn't refuse.

"I suppose I will, since he's already bought the ticket," she mumbled.

"Wonderful." Ruby clapped her hands like a young girl. "Run upstairs and freshen up. I'll do the dishes in a jiffy and we'll all meet at the front door."

Trent had the good sense not to make any teasing remarks. He remained silent as Rana left the room. In fifteen minutes they all gathered at the front door. Ruby, wearing red from her earrings to her sandals, was disappointed in Miss Ramsey's appearance. Ruby had hoped she would use the outing as an excuse to dress up. Instead, she looked more dowdy than ever in a shapeless pair of army-green slacks and a loose shirt that hung almost to her knees. Didn't the girl own anything more suited to the climate and the season, something airy and light and summery?

Even though her hair had been brushed, it hung closer to her face than usual, hiding everything except her lips, her nose, and those damned glasses. Ruby sighed in consternation, but refused to allow Miss Ramsey's disregard for fashion to spoil her own evening out.

She chattered gaily as Trent escorted them to Ruby's sedan, which they had decided to use since there wasn't room for the three of them in his low sports car. He opened the front passenger door and indicated that Rana should get in. Instead, she nudged Ruby forward. Before Trent could assist her, she had opened the back door, slid inside, and slammed the door behind her.

He only smiled as he walked around the back of the car and got into the driver's seat. She was angry. Good. The thawing of Miss Ramsey was going to be great fun.

The theater was crowded, and they were lucky to find three seats together. Rana went into the row first, knowing that Trent would allow his aunt to go before him.

Her ploy worked, but only temporarily. He was cagey. He excused himself to get refreshments during the previews of upcoming movies. When he returned with his hands full, he asked Ruby to switch seats with him, so that the tub of popcorn he had bought would be accessible to all three of them. Ruby did as he asked without argument, and

Rana found herself sitting beside him despite her earlier maneuvering.

He distributed the drinks, handed Ruby her box of chocolate candies, and also offered her the popcorn. "No, thank you, darling. It gives me gas."

Rana stifled a giggle, but almost choked on it when she felt the firm pressure of Trent's knee against hers. He spread wide his muscular thighs and wedged the bucket of popcorn between them.

Leaning close to her and touching her ear with his lips, he whispered, "Feel free to dig in any time."

She sniffed her disdain and kept her eyes resolutely on the movie screen. It was bad enough having his knee rubbing her leg and his elbow crowding hers on the armrest. There was no way she would grope between his thighs for popcorn!

She made no attempt to hide her aggravation, but he was impervious to it. In fact, each time she tried to move her knee away, his followed. He had her arm virtually pinned between his and the back of the armrest. To have wrested it free would have caused a commotion, so she left it there. She didn't want him to know she was even aware of the steely strength of his arm, or of its warmth, which spread through hers, into her breasts.

"Don't those tinted lenses make Clint look sickly?" he asked in a raspy whisper that sent chills down her arms.

"No."

"Why don't you take them off?"

"I can't see without them."

"Sure of that? They don't look that thick."

"I'm sure." Actually, they were just tinted glass, but even without makeup her eyes were striking enough to attract attention.

"You're not eating any popcorn."

"I don't care for any, thank you."

He inclined toward her. "I even brought napkins . . . on the outside chance that you don't want me to lick your fingers."

"Shut up!"

"Shhh!" "Shhh!" "Shhh!" The hissing came from several directions at once. Ruby leaned forward in her seat and gave them both a stern look. She mouthed, "Behave," before sitting back in her seat and returning her concentration to the movie.

"Now see what you did. You got us in trouble," Trent murmured after several moments had elapsed and everyone around them had settled back down.

"Me? You're the one who insisted I come to this damn movie," she whispered back fiercely. "Which reminds me, I'm mad as hell at you for manipulating me in front of Ruby. But you did and I'm here. You got what you wanted. Now the very least you can do is be quiet and let me watch the show."

"You want to watch the show?"

"That's the idea, isn't it?"

"Movie theaters aren't only for that, you know."

"What else are they for?"

"Illicit meetings. For doing naughty things in the dark. We could go to the back row of the balcony and neck."

That suggestion brought her head around. She stared up at him speechlessly. One side of his face was dark and inscrutable; the other reflected the light off the movie screen. His eyes were steady and compelling. He was smiling a half smile, an insinuating and sensual half smile. One of his dark brows was raised, indicating that his statement might have been an invitation that ended with, "Whaddaya say?"

He was handsome. Dangerously handsome. And he knew it.

Rana knew then that she didn't like him very much. In fact, she disliked him intensely.

She yanked her arm from beneath his on the armrest and turned her head back toward the screen. Readjusting herself in her seat, she made it impossible for his knee to reach hers.

Apparently he received her message loud and clear. He fell to watching the movie and munching popcorn in sullen silence. When the show was over, he politely escorted the ladies through the throng emptying from the theater, across the parking lot, and into the car. Ruby recapped the movie's plot, rehashed each action-packed fight, recounted every steamy detail of the love scene, and commented innumerable times on the star's appeal.

Rana remained silent in the backseat, counting the minutes until the evening would come to an end. As soon as they got through the front door of the house she said, "Thank you for the movie, Mr. Gamblin. Good night, Ruby."

"But I thought we all might enjoy a cup of tea together," Ruby said with a pout of disappointment. She wasn't finished dissecting the movie yet.

"Not tonight. I'm very tired. See you tomorrow." Coming on the heels of an already upsetting day, the excursion to the movie theater had left Rana physically tired and emotionally drained. And mad, she added as she closed the door of her apartment behind her. How dare he think he could get away with—

The knock on her door halted her bitter ruminations. Just as she'd suspected, it was Trent. And as usual, he was insolently propped against the doorjamb.

"Was it something I said?"

She crossed her arms over her chest. "No, it's what you *are*, Mr. Gamblin."

"Pray tell, what is that?"

"A conceited, spoiled, egomaniacal lecher. A self-centered, sexist, chauvinistic boor."

He whistled.

"I know your type, and I despise it. You think every female was designed solely to be your plaything, to be used and disposed of at your whim." She had his attention. He straightened up; the smug smile was no longer tilting up one corner of his mouth.

"Now, wait just a minute."

"No, *you* wait a minute. I'm not finished. You're the type who looks at a woman and automatically rates her appearance on a scale of one to ten. Don't deny it. I know it's true. You don't see a *woman*. You only see how she's packaged. And that's all that counts with you. You take none of her personality or intelligence into account, much less her feelings."

"I—"

"Look at me and look at you," she said, sawing her hand back and forth between them. "Knowing the kind of man you are, do you for one moment think that *I* think that you're interested in a romantic interlude with me? Well, I don't. I'm not that stupid. Nor am I naive enough to think that if you saw me on the street you'd be bowled over. You're coming on to me because I'm the only woman available.

"And even if you *were* interested, for whatever kinky reasons of your own, I'm not, and I take offense at your presumption that I would be. I'm sick of your juvenile innuendos and asinine suggestions. I find them in the poorest of taste. I wasn't put here on earth for your amusement, and I resent your thinking I was. If you think I can be washed overboard by your charm, by your good looks, or by your trite come-on lines, think again."

She planted her hands on her hips and glared up at him. "Where do you get off, making a toy out of a human being? You think of me only as a game to keep you occupied while you're here. Well, forget it. If it weren't for the fact that I like Ruby and don't want to hurt her feelings, I wouldn't even speak to you for the remainder of your stay. In summation, Mr. Gamblin, I think you're a class-A jerk."

She slammed the door in his face before he had time to utter a single word. She felt better than she had in months. Lord, it felt good to tell him off! At last she had vented a frustration with male attitudes that had been building for years.

Rana had found that men fell into three categories. There were those who were so intimidated by her beauty and success that they considered her unapproachable. Even if she sent signals that she might be interested, they didn't respond, because they simply couldn't or wouldn't compete with her.

Then there were those who dared to ask her out, but treated her like a fragile piece of porcelain, an objet d'art that might break if they didn't handle her with kid gloves. How could she ever develop a relationship with a man who considered her too perfect to touch?

Men who fell into the third category were the most prevalent and the most irritating. These were the ones who used her to decorate themselves. Since Rana was often photographed by paparazzi avid for candid shots of her—on the streets of New York, leaving a restaurant, entering a party, in the park eating an ice-cream cone—her escort also got the rewards of the free publicity she generated.

She had been courted by numerous politicians, rock stars, and businessmen, all of whom wanted to benefit from a well-publicized romance with Rana.

This type of man was the most manipulative and the most hurtful. He was the kind who saw nothing but her face and body and had little or no regard for the feelings of the woman inside the dazzling exterior. He used and used and used with malicious selfishness.

In a different but equally selfish way, Trent Gamblin was using "Ana" Ramsey. She was plain. She was pitiful. She was alone. No doubt he had decided to give the lonely spinster some kicks while he was in residence, give her something to liven up her colorless existence, give her something to write about in her diary, give her something to cherish and remember for all the lonesome years to come.

At the same time he would amuse himself. It would be a novelty to romance a woman so drastically different from the kind he usually had affairs with. It would be something to tell the boys in the locker room about when he returned. "Hey, guys, you can't believe how desperate she was for some lovin'."

How unconscionably selfish could one man be?

But Rana knew from experience that there was no limit to the extremes people would go to when using other people.

So tonight Rana had defended her alter ego, Miss Ramsey,

with a vengeance. It was a triumph over any man who had ever used any woman, beautiful or plain, simply because it suited him and she was convenient.

When she fell asleep, she felt cleansed. Why hadn't she developed that kind of backbone years ago? Why, after years of heartache and disillusionment, was she just now learning that the world wouldn't come to an end if she stood up for herself?

The next morning she was coming out of her bathroom, yawning and stretching, when the note was slipped under her door. Her arms, extended high above her head, froze there for a moment. She lowered them slowly and swallowed the next yawn as she stared at the single sheet of folded paper. She actually considered ignoring it. But her curiosity got the better of her. She crept forward and picked it up.

> *You're absolutely right. I behaved like a class-A jerk. I'm sorry. We can either sign a mutually agreeable truce, smoke a peace pipe, or go jogging together. I opt for the latter. I'd take it as a sign of forgiveness if you'd join me. Please.*

It wasn't signed, but then, how many people had she called a jerk lately? And that dark, heavy, masculine scrawl could only belong to one person.

In spite of her anger with him last night, she smiled. She refolded the note and went to the open window. She stared out, not really seeing the dew-sparkled grass or the landscape that simmered with the promise of another hot, muggy day.

He had had the good grace to offer an apology. Could she do less than accept it?

It was very early. The sun was just coming up, and the outdoors smelled new and fresh. A run on the beach would feel good. The exercise would limber up her body and her mind, so that when she settled down to work today, the creative juices would be flowing.

Before she could talk herself out of it, she flew to her closet and took out jogging clothes. She dressed, hastily tied her shoes on, put on her glasses, and rushed to open the door of her apartment before he gave up and left without her.

He was waiting quietly in the hallway, contemplating the toe of his worn running shoe. His dark gaze strayed from his shoe to her.

"Hi." His voice was wary.

"Good morning."

He took her attire as a good sign. She was wearing a gray sweat suit—as ill-fitting and baggy as everything else she owned—running shoes, and an Astros baseball cap. Trent tried to imagine a scenario in which he would whip off her glasses and she would shake her head and become a stunning sexpot, as the plain librarians in B movies always turned out to be. He sincerely doubted such a metamorphosis was possible in this instance.

"Ready to run?" he asked.

"It looks like a great morning for it. Not too humid."

"Compared to what?" he asked, wiping his brow, which was already damp with perspiration.

"Compared to a Brazilian rain forest."

He grinned, and nodded toward the stairs. "After you. And I give you fair warning, that's the last head start you'll get today."

They decided to drive the several blocks to the beach. He frowned at the choking, sputtering, clanking noise her used compact car made when she started it, but he went along with her suggestion to take it. The salty mist at the beach couldn't do much damage to its paint job.

They began their workout by doing some stretches. He was amazed to find her so agile and graceful as she methodically went about the warm-up procedure. She could bend at the waist and touch the ground flat-handed without groaning and grimacing. He wished she weren't so covered up. The gray sweat suit was really ghastly, but he could tell that no matter how it was shaped, her body was supple.

"So are we friends?" he asked as he executed some deep knee bends.

Rana diverted her eyes from his muscular thighs. "Do you want to be friends?"

He spread his feet wide and bent at the waist, walking his hands backward along the ground between his legs. "I want to be friends." When he came up, his face was flushed; she didn't know if it was from exertion or embarrassment.

"Then I guess we're friends," she said, smiling.

He nodded, but he was gently gnawing the inside of his jaw in what appeared to be perplexity. His brows were furrowed. "Maybe you should know something first."

"What?"

"I've never been friends with a woman before."

They stared at each other for a long, telling while. The beach was deserted at this time of morning. It wasn't yet time for young mothers to bring out their children for a few hours' diversion from the household routine, or for teenagers to cluster in groups and share tubes of tanning lotion and blasting radios, or for families on vacation to open up picnic baskets and argue over the day's agenda of activities.

Trent and Rana were alone. They were surrounded by silence, except for the occasional squawking of seagulls that swooped down into the gulf for breakfast, and the waves that broke on the shore in lacy, foamy, incessant patterns.

"Never?" Rana asked in a faint voice.

He squinted against the new sun as he pondered her question and searched his memory. "Nope. Never. When I played with Rhonda Sue Nickerson, the little girl who lived next door to us, I always wanted to play 'house,' so that, as the 'daddy,' I could kiss her good-bye when I left for 'work.' "

"How old were you?"

"Six or seven, I guess. When we got to be eight, I suggested playing doctor."

"Even at that age you were manipulating women."

He looked chagrined, and nodded. "S'pose so. I've never thought of a woman in any terms other than sexual."

"Well, our friendship will be a new experience for you."

"Right!" He raised his arms, holding his elbows parallel to the ground, and twisted at the waist. After a moment he stopped and looked at her, again with a puzzled expression. "How do you . . . uh . . . do it?"

"How do you do what?"

"Be friends with a woman."

She laughed. "The same way you're friends with anybody."

"Yeah?"

"Yeah."

"Race you to the pier!" He took off at a dead run. Surprised, she stood still for only a few seconds, and then she struck out after him.

"I won!" he exclaimed as he reached the first piling. He was barely winded.

"You cheated!"

"That's the way I've always done it with my buddies."

"Leave it to you to take full advantage of our new

friendship." She tossed her head back and laughed. He noticed that her top four front teeth were slightly crooked. He found the flaw endearing.

"Know what, Ana?"

"What?" She slipped off one shoe and shook sand out of it.

"I like you."

Her head snapped up and her bare foot dangled a few inches above the sand. "You sound surprised."

He laughed. "I guess I am."

"That's because I'm a woman, yet you're seeing past what I look like on the outside."

"It's a shame that people let appearance count for so much, isn't it?"

She bent down to replace her shoe. "Yes, it is," she murmured quietly. She guessed that he was thinking Ana Ramsey had been denied happiness because she was plain. Little did he or anyone else realize that beauty could bring its own kind of unhappiness.

"Did you let me win?" he asked suspiciously.

"Sure."

"That's sexist, too, you know."

"Our friendship is so new, I didn't want anything to upset the balance." She cocked her head to one side and smiled. If it had been any woman other than Ana Ramsey, Trent would have thought she was flirting.

"Ready to do some distance?"

"You betcha."

He set out at a run, and she fell into step with him. Before they had gone far, she realized just how outclassed she was. She waved him on, panting, "Go ahead, take your time, I'll wait here," before collapsing onto the hard-packed sand.

It was almost a half hour before he returned. He cooled down, jogging in ever-smaller circles around her, before finally dropping down beside her.

"If I had a lily to stick in your hands, you'd be the picture of a cartoon corpse," he teased. She was lying flat on her back, ankles crossed, hands folded over her tummy.

"Be quiet. I'm napping."

"Good idea." He lay down and stretched out beside her. "The sand's still cool."

"Feels good, doesn't it?"

"Uh-huh."

He studied her profile. Rolling to his side, he propped his hand in his palm. "I think there's more to you than meets the eye."

Stunned by his words, she turned her head. "What?"

"I think there's some deep, dark mystery lurking in your past."

"Don't talk crazy." She turned her face skyward again.

"Some sadness."

"No more than most people experience."

"What are you doing sequestered in my aunt's house, Ana?"

"What are you doing there?"

"You know what I'm doing there—letting my shoulder heal. I was living too hard in Houston, not getting enough rest."

"Why didn't you just discipline yourself?"

"I've got a weak character."

She laughed softly at his confession. "When Ruby told me you'd be staying temporarily, I thought you were probably hiding from a greedy ex-wife and her divorce lawyer."

He noticed that her breasts moved slightly when she laughed. Once a sexist, always a sexist, he thought ruefully. But, hell, he was a man, wasn't he? "I've never been married."

"No?" she asked, looking at him again.

"No. How about you?"

"I was married. Years ago. When I was very young."

That surprised him. And more than mildly. He was even more certain than ever that there was more to this woman than she let on. "Hm."

She rolled to her side to face him. " 'Hm.' How eloquent. But you can forget what you're thinking."

"What am I thinking?"

"That I'm nursing a broken heart and trodden spirit because a rotten husband did me wrong."

"Isn't that the way the song goes?"

"Not in this case. When my marriage was dissolved, it was by mutual agreement, a decision based on what was best for both of us."

"Then you still haven't answered my question, although I congratulate you on trying your damnedest to sidetrack me. What are you doing in hiding?"

"I'm not in hiding!" The vehemence of her protest betrayed just how accurately he had hit the target.

"Come on, Ana. An intelligent, attractive, talented woman like you doesn't take up residence in a boardinghouse with an elderly lady unless she's forced to do so."

"I wasn't forced. It's by choice that I'm here. And you didn't think I was attractive until this morning, when you decided to be my friend rather than an oversexed nuisance."

"I've always thought you were attractive." As he spoke the words aloud, he realized they were true. In the strictest sense of the word, he had been attracted to Ana Ramsey from the moment he'd first seen her. "All right, granted, your clothes leave a lot to be desired," he said in response to her dubious expression, "and you're not . . . not . . . ."

"Pretty," she supplied bluntly, enjoying his discomfiture.

"Not in the classical sense, no. But I like being around you. And don't start in on that sexist, chauvinist junk again. I'm complimenting you in a purely platonic way. I like being with you. I'm relaxed with you in a way I can't be with any other woman of my acquaintance, because I'm under no pressure to maintain my macho image. Do you know what a pain that is to live up to?"

"I can imagine," she said distractedly. She, of all people,

knew what it was to live up to an image, but her mind wasn't on that . . . because at that moment she realized that they were lying face to face on the lonely beach very much like lovers. Her body was feeling mellow and warm. And seconds before he had complained about having to live up to a macho image, she had been thinking just how beautiful his muscular body was.

She liked the tangy smell of his healthy sweat mingled with the salt air, liked the tumbled disarray of his wind-tossed hair, liked the way individual grains of sand clung to his damp skin. Her mouth went dry as her eyes traced the pattern of his chest hair. It swirled around neat, flat nipples and spread over his chest like a dark net.

"Well, it's a real pain," he continued, unaware of the delicious tingling his body was causing in her tightening nipples. "Because I'm a single, professional jock with a swinger's reputation, every woman I'm around expects me to . . . well, *perform*. It's nice to have somebody like you just to talk to." He raked his hand down his face. "Jeez, talk about a jerk. Don't I sound like one now? It's just that I don't remember a time I've lain in the sand with a woman and not made love to her."

The forbidden, unthinkable idea took hold as they lay there looking at each other. Even if their bodies didn't participate, their minds indulged, engaging in erotic fantasies.

She thought about touching him, about laying her hands on his chest and moving her fingers through his fleecy chest hair.

And he thought about slipping his hands beneath the top of her gray sweat suit and discovering the shape of her breasts.

She thought about the brevity of his shorts and what was beneath them.

And he thought about kissing her, of introducing his tongue into her mouth to see what she tasted and felt like.

She thought about him rolling her to her back and covering her with his hard, powerful body, entwining his legs with hers.

And he thought about rolling her to her back and covering her tall, slender frame, entwining his legs with hers.

Suddenly the mental images began to have profound physical effects that were too much for either of them to bear.

He reacted first, jumping to his feet and extending his hand to help her up. She looked at his hand for a hesitant moment before accepting it.

His long, hard fingers, accustomed to grasping a football, wrapped around her hand and held it as they strolled back to the car. He kept the conversation lively and jocular, because he felt guilty about thinking of her as a sex object.

Mentally Rana shook herself, forcibly shrugging off the sexual arousal that had held her captive. She and Trent were buddies, friends, pals. That was what she had wanted, what she had demanded. No entanglements with men for Rana. Uh-uh. And for Miss Ramsey, such romantic notions were out of the question.

Trent paid lip service to seeing past a woman's looks now, but in a week or two, when that virile body got hungry, he wouldn't select a Miss Ramsey to satisfy its sexual appetite.

"What are you going to do today?" he asked as they entered the cool, dim foyer of the house after the short drive home.

"Work, work, work." She shook her index finger just beneath his nose. "And don't you dare try to distract me today."

"Some friend you are. I thought we might—"

"Trent," she said threateningly.

"Okay, okay, scram." He hitched his chin toward the head of the stairs.

"Hello, dears," Ruby said, coming through the dining room upon hearing them. She was wearing a daisy-patterned apron over her jeans. "Miss Ramsey, the telephone is for you. I told the gentleman to hold when I heard you coming in. Trent, I've got your juice ready in the kitchen."

Rana raced up the stairs and answered the extension in her apartment. "Hello," she said breathlessly.

"Rana, hi, it's Morey."

"Hi," she said, glad to hear from him. "How are you? How's your blood pressure?"

"You can lower it. You can come back to work."

Four

I can't, Morey. Not now."

"Then, when?"

"I don't know. Maybe never."

"Rana, Rana." He spoke her name with a heavy sigh. "Haven't you proved your point yet?"

"You make my leaving sound like a child's pouting spell. I assure you my reasons for giving it all up went much deeper than that."

"I didn't mean to make light of it. Living with your mother would be like sharing a den with a barracuda." Rana was fully aware that there had never been any love lost between her mother and Morey. Susan had always held the agent in contempt, but had viewed him as a necessary evil she must tolerate for the furtherance of Rana's career. "What did she do that finally sent you over the edge? It must have been a dilly of a stunt."

Morey couldn't know what a painful, shameful memory he had evoked.

"All I'm asking is that you be nice to him, Rana. You're such a strange girl," Susan Ramsey had said in exasperation. "Any other girl would be beside herself if Mr. Alexander paid some attention to her."

"Then let 'any other girl' marry him."

"Who said anything about marriage?"

"I know you, Mother. You wouldn't be foisting Mr. Alexander off on me if matrimony hadn't entered your mind. And it doesn't have anything to do with morality. You're just too good a bargain hunter to settle for less."

"Would marriage to the owner of one of the largest cosmetics empires in the world be so terrible?" she asked sarcastically. "Think of what such an alliance would mean to your future."

"And to *yours*, Mother."

"I'll take none of your sass! Now, Mr. Alexander called, and his car is picking you up at eight. He sent this lovely diamond bracelet for you to wear tonight. Please go get dressed."

The bracelet had been the last straw, the final insult. "I'm not a prostitute," Rana had informed her mother calmly, but coldly. "Mr. Alexander can keep his diamond bracelet and I'll keep my self-respect."

Instead of getting dressed to go out with a man old enough to be her grandfather, she had packed a few meager belongings and left the Manhattan penthouse without another word.

During the lengthy bus trip south, she had tried to recall her mother's thousand and one machinations, but that was a futile exercise. For as long as Rana could remember, Susan Ramsey had had a hand in the small of her daughter's back, pushing Rana into things she didn't want any part of. How she had hated those beauty pageants for children, the modeling classes, the photography sessions, the endless rounds of interviews that always left her feeling embarrassed for both of them.

Susan had been tireless in her efforts to turn Rana into the perfect little girl, then into the perfect ingenue, then into the perfect woman . . . the woman Susan had always wanted to be herself. Psychologists would have had a field day with their relationship. If ever there was a case of a parent living vicariously through a child, this was it.

Rana was a hapless victim of Susan's ambition. Her father had been killed in an accident when she was an infant. There was no system of checks and balances within the family. Rana was forced to go along with Susan's plans. Rebellious outbursts had been few and far between. Patrick, the courageous sweetheart she had coerced into marrying her, had been one. That act of defiance had ended in heartbreak of such proportions that Rana hadn't risked another.

Susan had proved to her daughter just how ruthless she could be, and resignedly Rana had followed wherever Susan led. Until Mr. Alexander. Would her mother actually consider selling her into a marriage of convenience? The idea had jarred Rana into taking stock of her life. She had reached the conclusion that Susan wasn't ever going to change. If Rana wanted to alter her life, the change had to come from within herself. Leaving her mother and her career in New York had been the healthiest decision she'd ever made.

"It wasn't only Mother. It was me," she explained to her agent now. "I'm sorry that you had to be involved, too, Morey. Please understand. I had to get away from all that. And I'm having a wonderful time. I went jogging on the beach this morning. You should have seen me. Baseball cap, sweat suit. I look wretched, but I feel wonderful about myself. I'm peaceful. I'm free. For the first time in my life, I'm doing what *I* want to do."

"But does it have to be so drastic, sweetheart? Couldn't you just tell Susan to butt out once and for all?"

"Do you honestly think she would?"

He evaded that question and asked another. "Have you seen the undies ad?"

"By accident. I nearly died of shock."

"So have the hotshots of the company who peddle the stuff. They can't believe their ad people shelved the campaign for all these months. They're head over heels, Rana. Their sales have skyrocketed just in the week the ad has been out. You're decorating billboards all over the country. They want to do a series of television commercials."

"Using me?"

"Sure, using you. So the commercials will tie in with the

print ads. They think, and I agree, that you can do for simple cotton underwear what Brooke Shields did for blue jeans."

"I'm glad the ad is a success, Morey, but I don't want to go back to work."

"Not even to the tune of four hundred thou for a two-year contract?"

"You're kidding." Her legs folded beneath her, and she collapsed onto the rug.

"I see I've finally got your attention. I didn't say we'd accept four hundred. I'll counter with six hundred and I think we'll get an even half a million. How does that sound?"

"Ridiculous."

He chuckled. "Not so ridiculous. I could use the bread."

Her lips puckered with worry. "Have you been gambling again? Did you overextend?"

"Never mind my vices. You sound like my ex-wife. When are you getting your tush on a plane back to New York?"

She caught a glimpse of herself in the cheval glass in the corner. The woman sitting Indian fashion on the floor of the tidy, but modest, apartment didn't even resemble the model in the magazine ad. She was chubby by comparison. Her dark red hair hadn't been conditioned or trimmed in months. Her hands were a nightmare, with their square, short nails and paint-stained fingers. Her four crooked front teeth made for a less than perfect smile.

"I'm not coming back, Morey," she said softly, hoping he could sustain the blow. "I'm in no shape to. They wouldn't want me. I'm twenty pounds heavier than when you last saw me. I couldn't model underwear if I wanted to."

"So we'll send you to a fat farm for a couple of weeks. What'll it be, the Greenhouse or the Golden Door? You're closer to the Greenhouse. Want me to make you a reservation?"

"Morey, you're not listening. I'm not coming back. I don't want to."

The following silence was long and rife with tension. "Will you at least think about it?" Morey said finally. "It's a heck of a contract to turn down. We'll start slow, if you like. We'll accept no other work but this. Half a million is a helluva lot of money, Rana."

"I realize that," she said miserably. She didn't want Morey to suffer any financial setbacks because of her decision. "Don't think I'm not flattered or grateful. I am. But I have another life here. And I'm liking it."

She glanced at the door, thinking suddenly of the man across the hall. It unnerved her that thoughts of him should come to her mind at just that moment. He certainly had no bearing on her decision to stay in Galveston.

"Well, they're in a hurry, but I've stalled them. I told them you were taking an extended vacation, just as I have all our other clients. I'll give you a few days to sleep on it and call you back Friday."

"All right." She shook her head dismally. Her answer would be the same in a few days, or even in a few weeks, but she supposed it would be kinder to let him down gently than to refuse outright. His references to money made her uneasy. Morey had an almost compulsive penchant for betting on the outcome of any sporting event. "How's everything else in your life?"

"Fine, fine. Don't worry about me."

"Business is good?"

"Are you kiddin'? I've got Rana for a client and now everybody wants me as an agent."

She was relieved. Morey's agency had been handling showroom and catalog models when Rana and Susan walked through his door. When Rana's career had taken off, he had moved uptown in more ways than one. Soon he had more clients than he could handle, and had hired several assistants. Rana would always be glad that her success had contributed to his.

"Well, good-bye, then. Take care of yourself. Watch that blood pressure. Don't forget to take your medicine."

"Yeah, yeah. Good-bye. Think about the contract, Rana. Give it serious thought."

"I will. Promise."

She replaced the receiver thoughtfully. Something wasn't right. She could sense it. Was Morey taking care of his health? She was afraid he wasn't, now that she wasn't there to nag him about smoking too much and eating properly. She hoped he wasn't too affected by her decision to leave the business.

Her musings disturbed her, and she welcomed the interruption of a knock on her door. She leaped up to answer it, swearing to herself that her heart hadn't accelerated with the hope that it might be Trent. She had almost reached the door when she realized she wasn't wearing her glasses, and hurriedly put them on before opening it.

"Can you come out and play?"

He couldn't have looked more adorable. His hair was still damp and tousled from his shower. He had on athletic shorts and a ratty T-shirt with holes in it. He was barefooted, and the Band-Aid was still wrapped around his little toe.

With the same kind of affection Ruby had for him, Rana wanted to pinch him on the cheeks or on the bottom. He was just so damn cute. And far too much of a temptation. He was like an ice-cream cone to a dieter. One taste, and resolve flew out the window.

"No, I can't," she said firmly.

"Aw, please."

She giggled at his wheedling tone. "I can't. I've got to work. Don't you have anything constructive to do?"

"I could go to a gym and do a light workout with weights. Or I could do Ruby the favor she asked and sweep out her greenhouse. She wants to plant some flowers in there." He winked at her. "But my arm could be twisted to goof off."

"Well, mine couldn't be, so good-bye."

"Some friend you are turning out to be," he muttered as he wheeled to go.

Rana was smiling when she closed her door. She told herself her well-being was due to an overall good feeling about her life. But she wasn't convinced that Trent Gamblin didn't have something to do with it.

Each day of that week passed in a similar manner. It became their routine to meet and run together every morning. Ruby usually had breakfast waiting for them, which Rana ate before rushing up to her room to work while the morning light was still good.

Generally Trent made a nuisance of himself, but Rana was good-natured about it. It was almost impossible to get angry with him. During the day he did odd jobs around the house for Ruby. Their evenings were usually spent in the parlor watching television or playing board games. One evening the three of them strolled around the block. Ruby filled them in on the gossip concerning almost every family. No one had skeletons that Ruby didn't know about.

Another night, Trent got out the ancient, hand-crank ice-cream freezer, which he fondly remembered from his youth. He cleaned it, oiled its rusty crank, and asked Ruby to whip up some vanilla ice cream. A few hours later they were enjoying the homemade confection beneath the trees in the backyard.

Rana compared that tranquil evening to many she'd spent club-hopping in New York. She wouldn't have traded.

Trent couldn't remember a time when he had felt so relaxed and content in the company of a woman.

On Thursday Rana noticed she was low on supplies,

and went to the art store to stock up. When she returned, she was carrying a package so large and cumbersome she could barely see over it. As she set it down on her work-table, she was confronted with a startling sight.

A man was reclining on her bathroom floor. She couldn't see his head and shoulders, because they were inside the cabinet underneath the sink. But Rana recognized the shape of those muscular legs immediately.

"If you're a thief, I think it's only fair to tell you that I don't hide my precious jewels in the plumbing."

"Smart—"

"What was that?" she asked mischievously, propping her shoulder against the bathroom door.

"Never mind."

"I'm sure there's a logical explanation for why you're stretched out on my bathroom floor with your head under the sink."

"Ruby said you've been complaining about a leak down here."

"I have, but I thought she'd get a professional plumber to fix it."

He slid out far enough to peer up at her with a perturbed expression. "You're too picky—did anyone ever tell you that? I'm repairing your sink, all right?" He ducked his head back into the cabinet.

"Well, I should hope so. The drip ruined a bag of cotton balls."

"Yeah, I found a few soggy refugees."

"What's that smell?"

"Remember the bottle of disinfectant you had stored down here?"

"You didn't?"

"I did, but it wasn't my fault, because the lid wasn't screwed on tight enough. And what are you complaining about? You're not down here breathing the stuff."

Since he couldn't see her, Rana treated herself to a visual feast of his body. He was wearing denim cutoffs again, which seemed to be his uniform for the summer. His shirt had once been a sport shirt, but the plaid had faded until the pattern blurred together in spots. The sleeves had been cut out long ago. Now loose threads clung to the sweat-damp, tanned skin of his biceps. He had left the shirt unbuttoned. The sides had fallen open, leaving his chest bare.

Rana swallowed with difficulty. His arms were stretched above his head. Each time he moved, the muscles of his chest plumped up. His flat stomach was concave beneath his rib cage. His navel lay within a tantalizing nest of dense, dark hair.

A good two inches beneath it was the snap of his cutoffs. They were faded and threadbare and conformed softly to the shape of his lower body. Rana couldn't draw her eyes away from the spot where his thighs came together. His knees were raised. In the narrow strip of his lap, there lay a wrench.

"Ana?"

She jumped guiltily and yanked her eyes back to the opening beneath the sink.

"Yes?"

"What's the matter?"

"Nothing."

Could he detect her breathlessness? Why was she breathless in the first place? She had seen men, models, wearing next to nothing. Remember that swimsuit layout in *Bazaar*, the one that was photographed in Jamaica? her rational self asked her. Yes, she remembered those long-limbed, teak-colored, gorgeous male models with whom she had assumed such intimate-looking poses. But none of them, no male body, had ever stirred her senses the way Trent Gamblin did.

"Hand me that wrench, will you, please?"

"The wrench?"

"Yeah, both my hands are occupied. See it there?"

She saw it, all right, resting right against the fly of his cutoffs.

"Ana?"

"What?"

"Did you succumb to the fumes of the disinfectant?"

"No, I . . . uh . . ." She dropped to her knees beside him and extended her hand. It was shaking. She clenched her fist. Just pick up the damn wrench, pass it to him, and stop being such a ninny, she admonished herself. She thrust her hand forward, but a second before she grasped the wrench, she closed her eyes.

That proved to be a mistake. She miscalculated her reach, overshot her mark, touched the bare skin of his belly, and missed the wrench. A certain amount of desperate groping was required before she located it.

Trent became perfectly still, but a tremor shimmied through his body. Rana clutched the wrench and poked it into the cabinet.

"Here."

Clumsily he took the wrench from her. She withdrew her hand so quickly, it might have just escaped the jaws of a man-eating lion.

"Thanks." His voice was husky.

"You're welcome." Her voice was husky too.

"I'll be finished here in a sec."

"No hurry." Blindly she scrambled to her feet. "I have some . . . uh . . . things to . . . I went . . . the art store." Before she could make an even greater fool of herself, she fled the bathroom.

She was all thumbs as she unloaded the sack of art supplies. He would think . . . he would think . . . heaven only knew what he would think.

He's so . . . full.

Would he think she had touched him on purpose?

Maybe you touched something else.

It had been an accident.

No, that couldn't have been anything else. You touched . . . Oh, Lord.

It could have happened to anybody.

Even when she heard him enter the room, she kept her back turned. "All done," he said.

"Good. Thank you."

"Ana?"

"What?"

She felt him move up behind her. She closed her eyes, not wanting his smell to be so achingly familiar, not wanting to feel the warmth emanating from him. She felt his hand on her shoulder, tentative at first, then firmer.

"Ana?" he whispered softly, his breath moving her hair.

It would be so easy. So easy to comply with the urging of his hand and lean back against him. So easy to lay her head on his hard chest. So easy to turn to him and run her hands down his arms, to lift her lips to meet his.

So easy . . . and so foolhardy.

She immediately squelched the desire rising within her and turned around. "I appreciate your help, Trent," she said curtly, "but as you can see, I'm awfully busy."

He stared at her, stunned by her formal tone and frigid expression. How could she not . . . ? His whole body was on fire. And she was pretending it hadn't happened. What the hell was this? He had a good imagination, but it wasn't *that* vivid, dammit.

He'd felt that fragile hand of hers touching him and he'd almost exploded. He wanted her. Bad. But if she could act as if nothing had happened, then he damn sure could!

"So sorry to have bothered you, Miss Ramsey. The next time I spend almost an entire afternoon repairing your sink, I'll try to be done with it and out of your way by the time you get home."

He reached the door in three angry strides and slammed it shut behind him.

Dinner that night was a tedious affair. Trent had dreaded it, and had almost informed his aunt that he would be going out. He was tired of this self-imposed exile. He longed for one of his raunchy and raucous Houston haunts. A good meal. A good deal to drink. A good and sexy female into whom to empty his frustration.

He needed a woman in the most elemental way. One who didn't make him think. One who cooed over him, laid her hands on him, and didn't pretend later that she hadn't. One who flattered him and whispered outrageously suggestive things in his ear. He didn't want intellect or companionship or—heaven forbid—friendship. He wanted sex. Period.

But Ruby had told him that she was making his favorite meal, stuffed pork chops, and he would have been a real heel to run out on her after that. So here he was, sitting in the shuttered, candlelit dining room, staring across the table at Ana, who looked as coolly remote as he was hotly sullen.

Ruby sensed the hostile undercurrents, though she couldn't imagine what had happened between the two young people. By the time dinner was over, she was distressed, and badly wanted a cup of her "herbal" tea. To keep Miss Ramsey from retreating upstairs, she asked her to brew the tea for her. And to keep Trent from doing the same, she complained about the thermostat on the air-conditioner and asked him to check it.

The three of them met in the parlor and settled down to watch a movie on television. Trent saw little of it. His eyes kept straying toward the woman curled up in the easy chair, watching the television screen through blue-tinted glasses that aggravated the hell out of him. Why couldn't she wear clear eyeglasses, like any normal woman? Or, better yet, contact lenses?

But then, he doubted that Ana Ramsey did anything conventional. She seemed determined to pick the garments that would flatter her tall frame the least. Baggy slacks, loose shirts, shapeless skirts. Her attitude annoyed him because she could be a presentable package if she'd only try fixing herself up a little. Why didn't she do something with her hair? He wanted to brush it away from her face so he'd have an unrestricted view of her face for once.

"My tea needs sweetening," Ruby muttered, and left her seat on the sofa to make a trip into the kitchen.

Trent didn't move, but stared broodingly at Rana as he slouched in the chair opposite hers. His eyes were hooded by glowering brows, but he could tell she knew he was staring at her. Occasionally, she would glance at him. He was glad she was uncomfortable. Served her right. Hadn't he been uncomfortable all afternoon because of her?

Ruby returned, bringing the unmistakable bouquet of Tennessee sour mash with her. The pendulum clock on the mantel ticked rhythmically. The canned laughter of a banal comedy intruded on the thick silence blanketing the three viewers.

Trent barely noticed any of it. He was trying to understand how he could have been so turned on by Ana. The women he knew fell into one of two groups—those he wanted to go to bed with and those he'd been to bed with, because all those in the former group eventually graduated to the latter.

His attentions weren't often spurned. If anyone called it quits, it was he. Tall or short, blond or brunette, rich or poor, no woman was spared rejection when he tired of her. Often she was left mystified as to the reason for the sudden breakup.

Ana Ramsey was unlike any other woman he'd ever met. And for the life of him he couldn't figure out why he was stewing over her. Her caress that afternoon had been accidental. He was certain of that. But it had happened. So, okay, she was embarrassed by it. Why be so defensive? Why not just go with the flow?

If any woman ever needed a good, rowdy tumbling, it was Ana Ramsey. And from the top of his head to the tip of his toes, his body was telling him he'd been far too long without a female beneath him. To his way of thinking, they were prime candidates for hours of uninterrupted bedroom frolic.

At least now he knew something about himself that he'd always suspected. He couldn't be friends with a woman. To hell with being a chum. That stank. He'd tried it, and it hadn't worked. Because all he could think about tonight while he sat staring at the aloof Miss Ramsey was what she would look like naked.

"Do you think she's all right?"

"What?" At the unexpected sound of Ana's voice, he roused himself. Had his sulkiness been rewarded? Finally she had deigned to look directly at him and speak, something she had avoided doing all evening.

"Do you think Ruby's all right?" she repeated, indicating the older woman with a nod of her head.

Trent looked at his aunt. How long had her head been bent over her chest like that? And why hadn't he noticed her loud snoring before now? Because his mind had been too preoccupied with Ana, that's why.

He smiled. "I think she had one too many cups of tea." Rana smiled back. It was a pretty smile, despite her overlapping front teeth. He barely even noticed that flaw now.

"Should we waken her?" she asked him.

"That might embarrass her."

"You're right." She stood up and switched off the television. The absence of the blue-white light made the room much darker. Through the heavy shadows, Rana moved toward the sofa where Ruby sat sleeping. Trent got to his feet.

"Do you think you could carry her to her room?" She tilted her head back to look up at him.

"I think I can manage that."

For a moment neither moved. They just stood there, staring at each other through the darkness. Ruby's soft snores kept time with the clacking pendulum of the clock. The room closed in around them. It was difficult to breathe.

They were hot all over.

Rana was the first to move and break the spell. "Can you lift her up?"

"Sure."

Trent was glad for a chance to expend energy. If he didn't find an outlet for it soon, he'd explode. He bent down and slid one arm beneath his aunt's knees, the other behind her back. Seemingly without any effort, he lifted her up. He grimaced.

Rana laid her hand on his upper arm. "Does that hurt your shoulder?"

"It's all right." He glanced down at her hand.

She removed it. "I didn't think about your shoulder, or I never would have suggested that you carry her."

"Why don't you go ahead and turn down her bed?"

Hurriedly Rana did as he asked. Ruby's apartment was

located down the central hall, past the staircase, at the back of the house. It was cluttered with a lifetime of memorabilia. The bedroom had a small bath adjoining it. Her living quarters were actually smaller than those of her tenants. Rana peeled back the crocheted bedspread and the sheets. Trent laid his aunt gently on her bed. She hadn't awakened.

"Thank you. I'll undress her," Rana offered.

He was surprised. He couldn't imagine any of the women he knew doing such a thankless task. He felt immediately ashamed of himself. All afternoon and evening he'd been harboring a grudge against this woman, mentally accusing her of being everything from a dried-up old prude to a heartlessly fickle tease.

If he had reacted so violently to her accidental touch this afternoon, what must she have felt? Mortification, to say the least. Now, here she was, offering to undress a tipsy old lady out of sheer kindness.

A strong new emotion welled inside him. It was so powerful he couldn't allow himself to speak. He merely nodded and left the room.

When Rana followed him several minutes later, she was surprised to find him waiting in the hall. "Everything okay?"

"Yes. She didn't miss a snore."

They walked through the house. He switched off lights as they went. His footsteps fell close behind hers on the stairs. When they reached the doors of their respective rooms, they faced each other awkwardly. A faint light was cast by one small bulb at the end of the hall.

He wanted to touch her. God, he wanted to. He wanted to lay his palm against her cheek just to see if it was as soft as it looked. He wanted to thread his fingers through the thick mane of hair hanging down her back, to sweep it away from her face so he wouldn't feel as though he was looking at her through a screen. He wanted to take off her eyeglasses and look into her eyes, to see their color, to solve the mystery of them. He wanted to explore beneath her bulky clothing with his hands, to find the breasts that haunted his imagination. He wanted to run his tongue along those beguiling front teeth.

And his body was informing him that he wanted to be much more intimate with her than he was allowing himself to contemplate.

"Good night, Ana," he said thickly.

"Good night, Trent."

In her room, Rana walked immediately to her bed and lay down. Her whole body was trembling. She had wanted so badly for him to touch her. *Touch me,* she had all but cried out.

But Ana Ramsey wasn't beautiful, and Trent Gamblin was accustomed to making love to beautiful women.

Making love? She scolded herself. *She* was the one who had wanted friendship. Now that she had that, did she want something more?

Honestly she had to admit that she didn't know. When

she was around Trent she felt either miserable or wonderful. Why? Her knees went weak at the sight of him. The sound of his voice elicited almost uncontainable excitement within her.

The worst of it was, she spent far too many hours each day thinking about him. That was dangerous and just plain stupid. One day soon he'd be leaving for his summer training camp. Then what? Then he'd get caught up again in his celebrity lifestyle. He would forget about her.

And it wasn't as if she didn't have enough problems of her own to occupy her. Tomorrow Morey would call, expecting her response to the contract they had been offered. Did she want to return to her life in New York? Did she want to become *the* Rana again? Wouldn't that be safer than falling in love with Trent? Was it wise to trade one set of problems for another? How many ways could a heart be broken?

No matter what her final decision, one thing remained certain: She must stay away from Trent. Starting tomorrow.

Five

When Trent came by the following morning for their run, she pretended not to hear his knock. Eventually he went out alone, and Rana breathed a sigh of relief. And disappointment. She had come to look forward to their morning jogging.

Carefully she pressed the wrap skirt she'd been working on, arranged it on a hanger, and covered it with a plastic bag. In all modesty she thought it was her best work, and hoped that it would meet with Mrs. Rutherford's approval.

Getting dressed didn't require near the time it once had. She washed her hair, but left it to dry on its own. She smoothed some moisturizing lotion on her tanned face— her mother had never let her swim or play on the beach when she was a child, because she didn't want Rana's skin to suffer the damaging effects of the sun—but left it free of makeup. She put on the blue-tinted eyeglasses and dressed in a shapeless, mud-colored sack dress, which she didn't even belt. Barry would be horrified. She went downstairs to eat a quick breakfast before leaving.

"Have you seen Trent this morning?" Ruby asked as she poured Rana a cup of coffee. Rana noticed that Ruby was moving carefully and wincing at any loud sound. Rana hid a secret smile behind her china coffee cup.

"No. Why?"

"He's in an awful mood. I thought maybe he clued you in while you were jogging."

"I didn't run this morning, because I was getting ready to go to Houston. I haven't seen him."

"Well, he's swelled up like a bullfrog. He came stamping in a few minutes ago from his run and wearing a face like a thundercloud. He went straight up to his room without even stopping to drink his fruit juice."

"Hm," Rana said noncommittally as she buttered a piece of toast. "Got up on the wrong side of the bed, I guess."

Was he pouting because she hadn't jogged with him? In some ways he was such a child. His childish streak aroused her maternal instincts, and she found herself smiling at this latest tantrum. But she immediately squashed that emotion, as she had all the others. She couldn't allow herself to feel anything for Trent. Where he was concerned, she had to be in an emotional vacuum.

"I've got to get on the road, Ruby," she said, hastily finishing her breakfast. "Don't look for me until late this afternoon."

"Good luck with your business, dear. And please drive carefully. The freeways are treacherous."

"I'll be careful." She kissed Ruby's cheek and left the house by way of the back door.

The detached garage, located on one side of the backyard, had been an addition to the original house. Rana was glad to see that Trent's sports car was parked behind Ruby's, so it wouldn't be necessary for her to ask him to move it. She hung the skirt on the hook in the backseat of her compact and climbed behind the steering wheel.

At first she thought nothing of the chugging, choking sound of the car's motor. It was always reluctant to start. But after several unsuccessful attempts to pump the engine to life, she began cursing it. The garage was airless and stifling, even this early in the day. She tried again, becoming more frustrated every second. She wasn't on a tight schedule, but she had to get to Houston today.

"Damn!" she cried, banging her fist on the steering wheel. Barry would have a fit if she failed to deliver the skirt today.

She retraced her steps to the back door. "Ruby," she called out, "is there bus service between Galveston and Houston?" She entered the kitchen to find Trent munching on a piece of crisp bacon. Ruby was holding an ice pack to her head as she sipped coffee.

The landlady put down the ice pack. "I thought you'd gone, dear."

Resolutely Rana kept her eyes away from Trent, who

was dressed in a sport shirt and slacks. There was a lightweight sport jacket draped over the back of his chair. "My car won't start. I'll have to take a bus to Houston. Where can I catch one?"

"I'm going to Houston today. I'll drive you," Trent said.

"What a dear boy," Ruby said, smiling fondly at her nephew. "Sit down, Rana, and have another cup of coffee."

"But," Rana protested, wetting her lips, "I really need to go alone."

She couldn't take Trent into Barry's store with her. Barry might blurt out something that would give her away. All night she had toyed with the idea of having Morey accept that contract. If she went back to work, she would avoid the heartache of getting more deeply involved with Trent. But if she made that decision, she wanted simply to disappear. She never wanted him to know she wasn't the plain Miss Ana Ramsey he thought her to be. If he ever found out about her other life, he would be furious with her for deceiving him.

"I'm probably going miles out of your way," she said discouragingly.

"Where do you need to go?"

"The Galleria."

"Fine," he said, with a "that's settled" nod of his head. "I've got to see a doctor about my shoulder. His office is near there. Are you ready?" he asked, standing up.

"Really, I can't trouble you," she said quickly, desperately.

"Look," he said, pulling his coat off the chair with an irritated yank, "I've got to go anyway. It would be crazy for you to try to get around Houston in a damn bus. Now, do you want to ride with me or not?"

No, she didn't want to. But realistically, she didn't have much choice. Lowering her head, she mumbled, "Thank you, yes, I'll ride with you."

They said their good-byes to Ruby, who repeated her instructions to drive carefully. In Trent's sports car, Rana folded the skirt in her lap.

"Sorry about that," he said, glancing down. "There's no place to hang it."

"It will be all right."

That was the extent of their conversation until they were halfway to Houston. Then she ventured to ask, "How is your shoulder?"

"Why didn't you run with me this morning?"

"I didn't have time. I was getting ready for my trip to Houston."

"And you couldn't bother to tell me that?"

"I must have been in the shower when you came by. I didn't hear your knock."

"I didn't hear the shower running, either."

"Are you in the habit of listening at my door?"

"Are you in the habit of lying?"

They lapsed into another turbulent silence, interrupted only by Trent's muttered curses at the sluggish Houston traffic.

After several minutes Rana became ashamed of both of

them for behaving in such a snippish, juvenile way. "How is your shoulder?" she asked again.

"I don't understand you, Ana," he shouted, as though he'd been sitting there fuming, waiting for the right moment to vent his anger, just as he waited for opportunities to whip his car around motorists driving too slowly to suit him. "You were justified in being mad at me when I kept coming on to you. So, all right, you slapped my hand and I admitted that I deserved it. I thought we were going to be friends, but you never lighten up. I never know where I stand with you. You're stiff and unbending and uptight. It's no surprise to me that your husband split and that you don't have any friends."

He guided the sleek car into one of the lanes leading to the massive shopping complex. "You can let me out here," Rana said tightly, her lips barely moving. She already had a grip on the door handle.

He braked the car to a screeching halt at the curb, and she got out after speaking a terse "Thanks."

"A couple of hours?" he asked.

"Fine," she said, and slammed the door behind her.

Barry didn't improve her mood. There were a few shoppers in the store, but they were being helped by his effusive sales staff. The moment he saw Rana come in, he grabbed her arm and hurried her to the rear of the store and into his office. Unlike the immaculate and serene shop, which was decorated in soothing pastels, his office was cluttered and cramped and reeked of acrid tobacco smoke. He faced her, folding his arms in a gesture of disapproval.

"My Lord, if anything, you've gotten worse."

"Don't start in on me, Barry," she said, hanging Mrs. Rutherford's skirt on a hook and collapsing into the only available chair. "I've already had a helluva morning."

"You look positively wretched."

"Thanks. That's the point. I wish to remain anonymous, something you make almost impossible by displaying a poster of that underwear ad in your lingerie section. How could you, Barry?"

"Because it sells panties, dear heart. Dozens of them. Believe me," he said, sliding appraising eyes over her with obvious distaste, "no one will recognize you. In fact, I shall do my best to keep you hidden. If my customers saw their idol, Ana R., they'd throw up their hands and scream. They may envision you as an eccentric artist, an image I've intentionally promoted, but they wouldn't want to know you're a ragpicker."

"Do you have a diet soda?"

"Yes," he said, opening a small refrigerator tucked under a sagging shelf, "but don't get too comfy. We have loads of business to discuss. By the way, the skirt is fab." He had lifted the plastic bag and inspected it. "Mrs. Rutherford will be absolutely giddy."

An hour and a half later, Rana stood up to leave, with a new idea to consider and a hefty check and four orders in her purse. "Luckily I have a supply of silks and cottons I got on my last visit to that warehouse," she told him. "Be sure to have your seamstress send me a list of the customers' measurements next week. The ones she personally takes, not the ones they submit themselves. Ladies tend to fudge in their own favor."

Barry took hanks of Rana's hair in each of his hands and pulled it back away from her face, holding it there as he studied her. "Ahh, just a glimpse of the old Rana. Why not let me send you down to Neiman's salon and have your hair and makeup done? Then I'll deck you out in that new Ungaro collection. Or I have a white silk jersey Kamali that's perfectly Rana. Do some floor modeling for me today, and my sales will soar. It would be good for both of us."

She shook her head, and he released her hair, regretfully watching it fall back to cover her classic cheekbones. "No, Barry."

"Will you ever go back to doing what you do better than anyone, love?"

"Morey wants me to." She told Barry about the two-year contract she'd been offered. "I haven't decided whether to accept it or not."

He sighed. "Are you happy this way, Rana?"

"Happy?" Had she ever been happy in her life? Was anyone? "I'm content. I think that's the most anyone can ask for."

Not wanting to become too maudlin, she kissed him, thanked him again for the orders, and assured him she'd think about his latest innovative idea. Once out in the mall, she realized that she hadn't specified a place to meet Trent. She didn't have long to ponder her dilemma, because she spotted him walking around aimlessly, occasionally stopping to watch the ice skaters gliding across the center rink.

He was so very attractive. Each time she saw him, she was mildly surprised all over again by how much he appealed to her. He wasn't bulky and massive like professional football linemen, but his muscles filled out his jacket and slacks. His clothes fit to a "T" and were well tailored, though casual. She liked the way his dark hair waved naturally, flirting with the tops of his ears and his collar. He was wearing opaque sunglasses, probably to keep fans from recognizing him.

She made her way toward him slowly, glad for the opportunity to study him without his knowing it. When she was still a fair distance away, he turned his head in her direction. He must have seen her instantly, because he began wending his way toward her through the crowd.

"I'm sorry, Ana." He spoke the words in a breathless rush as soon as he came within hearing distance. "What I said was—"

A harried lady shopper bumped into him from behind. Taking Rana's arm, he guided them out of the flow of foot traffic, placing her between him and the wall. She had to angle her head back in order to look at him. He took off his glasses and tucked them into the breast pocket of his coat. His dark eyes were troubled.

"What I said in the car just before you got out, well, it was unforgivable," he said. "I didn't mean it. I was just so damn mad."

"You don't have to apologize, Trent."

"Yes, I do. These are for you." He thrust a bouquet of daisies at her. "I wanted to get roses, but they were sold out. Forgive me? Please."

Tears filled her eyes as she stared wordlessly into the cluster of daisies. She lowered her face, nestling her nose among the dewy petals. She had been sent flowers often. Extravagant arrangements of roses and orchids had come from counts and corporate presidents. None had ever meant anything to her. This small, unpretentious bouquet of humble daisies was the most precious gift she had ever received.

"Thank you, Trent. They're lovely."

"I had no right to speak to you like that."

"I provoked you."

"Well, anyway, I'm sorry."

"Apology accepted."

The mall was crowded. Shoppers hurried past them. Still they didn't leave their spot. He continued to stare down at her.

"Have you been waiting long?" he asked.

"No. I saw you from across the atrium."

"I was so mad I didn't even tell you where to meet me."

"That's all right. We found each other."

"Yes. We found each other."

As he continued to gaze down at her, her words took on a deeper meaning. He inched closer. His hand came up to rest against her cheek. He whispered her name. Then he lowered his head and pressed his lips against her cheek.

Rana stopped breathing. She didn't move. The daisies, which she was holding against her chest, were crushed between them. She heard the crackling of the green tissue they were wrapped in and felt the damp petals against her arms.

But it was the man who captured most of her awareness. He smelled like summer sunshine and a masculine fragrance. She wanted to nuzzle his warm neck and breathe deeply of his scent. His lips went from cool to warm against her cheek. His breath, rapid and unsteady, whispered across her face. Only a supreme act of will kept her from flinging her arms around him and never letting him go.

He hesitated, as though trying to make up his mind about something; then he stepped away. "Let's get out of here," he said, taking her arm and leading her through the mall.

"How is your shoulder?" she asked once they were in the car and negotiating traffic again.

He laughed. "You've asked me that several times already."

"And I never got an answer. What did the doctor say?"

"He said that by the time I go off to summer training camp, I should be in great shape."

"Trent, that's wonderful," she said enthusiastically, tamping down a wave of sadness that came with his news. When he left for camp, he'd be leaving her life for good.

"I guess the rest and relaxation is starting to pay off." He grinned across at her. His smile showed brilliantly in his darkly tanned face. "Hungry?"

She nodded. "I didn't get any lunch."

"Neither did I."

He took her to one of his favorite Mexican restaurants. She had just begun to acquire a taste for the spicy ethnic cuisine. "Are you sure we'll get out alive?" she commented dubiously when he braked in the gravel parking lot of the restaurant. It hardly qualified as such. "Cantina" might have been a more appropriate description. The porch sagged considerably. The sign over the door was so faded that only a few letters were distinguishable. The windows were murky and decorated with window boxes containing dusty plastic flowers in garish colors.

"I didn't say it was fancy, only that it was the best."

They laughed and joked all through the meal, which Trent ordered from an enormously fat woman who kept patting him affectionately on the cheek and calling him *"Angelito."*

When they left the restaurant, he drove Rana around Houston, pointing out places of interest that an out-of-towner would rarely see.

By the time they returned to Galveston, it was well after dark. Ruby was waiting for them at the back door. "I've been worried," she said. "Trent, did you forget that you promised to take me bowling tonight?"

Rana could almost hear his inward groan, but for his aunt's sake, he smiled. "Of course not. Not after looking forward to it all week. Is it all right if Ana comes along?"

"Certainly," Ruby said. "The more the merrier."

Rana had had such a perfect day, she wanted it to stop now, before something happened to ruin it. Besides, she didn't want to intrude on Ruby's evening with her adored nephew. "I'm a lousy bowler. You two go ahead. I'm tired and want to get to bed early anyway."

She wanted to think that Trent was disappointed. He seemed to be as Ruby practically dragged him out the front door. "Be sure to lock up," he told Rana as she waved good-bye. She had the distinct impression that he would much rather have stayed with her than escort his aunt to the bowling alley. His farewell smile left a warm, glowing feeling inside her.

In her room, she placed the daisies in a vase of water and put them where she could see them as she reclined in a hot bubble bath. She had just stepped out when her telephone rang.

"Where have you been all day?" a gruff voice asked when she answered.

"And hello to you, too, Morey. I had to go to Houston."

"That's what your landlady told me."

"You'd be proud of the money I came home with."

"Too bad I'm not getting my percentage." Rana wondered again if Morey hadn't gotten himself into financial straits with his gambling, but before she could inquire, he plunged right into the business at hand. "Well, have you thought it over?"

"Yes, Morey."

"Spare me the suspense."

"My answer is no."

She had thought it over carefully, weighing every aspect of her decision. As recently as last night she had entertained the thought of returning to her former way of life, despite the unhappiness it would bring her.

But today, when Trent had presented her with the flowers, she'd realized how much progress she had made. A man had given her flowers without considering whether or not she was pretty. The daisies weren't a tribute to her beauty, but to the woman she was on the inside.

She didn't want to return to the superficial world, where she was considered a commodity solely because God had given her a certain face and body.

"Do you realize what you're passing up, Rana?"

"Please don't try to talk me out of my decision, Morey. My mind's made up. I'm not saying I'll never go back. Just not right now."

His sigh conveyed his disappointment, but all he said was, "That's it, then?"

"Yes. That's it."

They chatted about other things. She inquired about her mother's health. Morey described her mother's personality in crude terms, but assured Rana that Susan was in good health.

"She'll raise billy hell when I tell her you're turning this offer down. And since you're not here, she'll take it out on me."

"I know, and I'm sorry you'll bear the brunt of it."

"Goes with the territory."

"Are you terribly disappointed, Morey?"

"Disappointed, yes. I think you're a little crazy, but I still love you."

"And I love you too. I'm sorry to be such a burden."

"Life's full of them, Rana. Full of them."

They said their good-byes. Rana wished she felt more comfortable with her decision. Instead, her conversation with Morey left her feeling vaguely sad and homesick for him.

Then she spotted the bouquet of daisies. They were like a ray of light that penetrated her despondency and coaxed back her golden mood. It stayed with her until she finally dropped off to sleep.

She slept late. When she opened her eyes and glanced out the window, she could tell the sun was well up. Her clock verified the lateness of the hour. As soon as her feet hit the floor, she noticed the slip of paper lying just inside her door.

I knocked twice, but didn't hear a sound. Yes, I listen at your door often. Guess you're sleeping late. I approve. See you later.

The note was left unsigned, but the barely legible scrawl, as well as the humor, was dearly familiar.

She dressed and went downstairs. The house was deserted. She ventured into the backyard and decided to tour Ruby's greenhouse. The elderly lady had been bragging about the results of her efforts there.

It was hot and humid inside the glass building, but Rana enjoyed the smell of freshly turned soil. Not a breath stirred. Condensation collected in droplets on the panes of glass surrounding her. It was silent. The sound of her footsteps was absorbed by the spongy earthen floor. She walked between the long tables, with their neat rows of potted plants. She studied them, delighting in every exotic bloom, each delicate leaf, with its unique tracery of veins.

"Sloth is a sin."

"Oh!" she exclaimed, and spun around.

"I did it again, didn't I? I snuck up and startled you? Sorry. I didn't mean to."

Trent heaved a bag of peat moss off his shoulder and wiped his hands on the seat of his cutoffs. His T-shirt was damp with perspiration.

Rana smiled at him. "I know you didn't mean to. It's just so quiet in here. Good morning, by the way. Where's Ruby?"

"I just made her go in and lie down. We went to the nursery to pick up this peat moss. It's so hot and muggy, she got a little dizzy. I told her I'd finish her project."

"Which is?"

"To put those bedding plants into those pots," he said, pointing them out to her.

"Pretty begonias," Rana remarked as she rolled up the sleeves of her shirt. "I'll help."

"Don't feel that you have to."

"I want to."

As a child she'd never been allowed to play in the dirt. She had never been allowed to do anything that spoiled her perfection. Every hair had to be in place. She wasn't allowed to ride a bicycle or roller-skate because she might scrape her knee. Scabs or scars were to be avoided at all costs. As a teenager, she had rebelled occasionally, but when her little acts of defiance were discovered, her mother's wrath made the adventures hardly worthwhile.

Nor had she had many friends to play with when she was growing up. She had never been free to run with the other children in the neighborhood. During adolescence, female friends were rare, because other girls saw her extraordinary looks as a threat. What potential friend with any brains wanted to be compared to Rana?

Boys, on the other hand, had held her in awe, and she

had very few dates during high school. Rana Ramsey was the most gorgeous creature most of the boys in her school had ever seen. She was too intimidating a proving ground on which to test newfound manhood.

Now Rana seized this chance to play in the dirt. "What do I do first?"

"First you take off some clothes," Trent said.

"What!"

"You don't think that's a good idea?"

"No."

"Don't be shy. If it makes you feel any better, I'll take off some of mine too." He laughed at her withering glance. "Ana, you'll swelter in all those clothes. It's like a sauna in here."

"Oh, no, I'm fine."

"I'm afraid you'll melt and all that will be left is a pile of clothes nobody else will want and I'll be stuck with."

She glared at him, but it was all in fun. "Don't worry about me and my clothes and the heat, okay?"

He shook his head in bafflement, wondering if she had some hideous skin disease she didn't want anybody to know about. She had jogged with him each morning wearing a sweat suit that covered her from neck to ankles. "Okay, but if you faint from heat prostration, remember I warned you."

He showed her how to fill each container from a bag of potting soil and what proportion of peat moss to mix with it. Soon she was wielding the trowel as though she'd done it all her life. Occasionally she blotted her dripping forehead with her sleeve, but she didn't even notice the muggy heat, she was having so much fun.

"Do you mind?" Trent asked her after a while. He was holding the hem of his T-shirt.

"Uh, no."

He peeled it over his head and tossed it down. "I think I'm the one who's melting."

Rana, gazing at his bare torso, was experiencing her own melting sensation, but it was internal. Her thighs felt as though they were liquefying. "You certainly look fit enough to play football," she said as casually as her tight throat would permit. Muscles rippled beneath his supple brown skin with each movement of his arms and shoulders.

"I hope I am."

She noticed his worried frown and the hesitancy in his voice. "Do you have doubts?"

He laughed, but it wasn't a mirthful sound. "I've lived with that kind of doubt every season I've played professionally, and even before then when a championship was at stake."

"But you've had a spectacular career." When he looked at her inquiringly, she added, "Ruby's filled me in on it since you came here. Was that just her pride talking? Aren't you considered one of the best?"

Ordinarily he would have accepted such compliments as his due. But with Rana, he felt compelled to be honest. "I've had some good seasons, but last year was a disaster."

"Why, Trent?"

"I'm getting old."

She laid the trowel aside and gave him all her concentration. "Old? You're not even thirty-five."

"Which in professional football is well past middle age." Self-conscious about speaking aloud his innermost fears, he fiddled with a watering can. It was a relief, however, to have someone listen so carefully. For months he had needed to confide in someone. He couldn't have stopped the flow of words if he had wanted to.

"Last season my age began to catch up with me, though I'd been fighting it for several years before that. My elbow had to be operated on three years ago. Once I got that back in shape, my shoulder started to give out. Every time I threw a pass, it hurt like hell. I was hitting the receivers fewer times each game. Since we're basically a passing team, our offense was shot to hell. There was no one else to blame. The buck stops at the quarterback. In this case, me."

Rana knew nothing about football, but she could sympathize with what he was telling her. She had known models who had considered their lives over at thirty because they were too old to continue their careers.

She moved closer to him, and barely resisted the urge to lay a comforting hand on his arm. "Surely you knew when you started that it couldn't last forever."

"Of course I did. I'm not that unrealistic. I haven't walked around with my head in the clouds. I've made financial preparations for my retirement from football. I'm a silent partner in an extremely lucrative commercial real-estate firm in Houston. But I want to retire when I say I'm ready, not when I'm *forced* to. Each season new talent is recruited for the team. Lord, they're good, Ana. And so damn young." He shook his head ruefully. "You probably think I'm whining because I'm jealous of the younger guys. I swear that's not it."

"I believe you," she said softly.

He clenched his fists and closed his eyes. "I want just one more season. A winning season. I want to go out on top, not as an object of pity or derision."

Her hand found its way to him of its own accord, and she squeezed his arm to emphasize her heartfelt words. "No one would ever pity you, Trent. I think this *will* be your season. I know it."

"You do?"

She stared up at him earnestly. "Yes, I do."

Everything receded into the background. They were left in a universe of their own. She searched his face greedily, feeling the fear and insecurity behind his eyes as surely as she had felt her own so often.

If I weren't pretty, my mother wouldn't love me at all.

That was what the lonely, beautiful little girl had grown up thinking. Up until six months ago, she had continued to think that her only value came from the way she looked.

Since she had thrown off the Rana Look, she had culti-vated two important friendships, Ruby's and Trent's. She *was* a person worthy of love and friendship, no matter what she looked like.

For as long as she could remember, she had tried to be what her mother wanted. She had wanted Susan's approval desperately, but she had always fallen short of her mother's expectations.

"Stand up straight, Rana. . . . Don't slouch, Rana. . . . Is that a pimple, Rana? Honestly! I've taught you how to clean your face, but you don't do it. . . . Are you wearing your retainer? Do you want crooked teeth? . . . You wrin-kled your dress, after I spent a half an hour ironing it."

And even when Rana had been as close to perfect as any human being could possibly be, Susan could always find fault.

Yes, Rana could identify with Trent's anguish and un-certainty. In his drive to succeed on the gridiron, it didn't matter what pieces of him were left behind on the Astro-turf, what bones were broken, what muscles were sprained, what pain he endured. He was a competitor. He would always go the distance, give his all. But because his very best might not be good enough, he was suffering a private hell.

"Thanks for saying that," he said softly.

His eyes didn't waver from her face. The air was thick with desires long suppressed. His body felt heavy and feverish with an emotion he couldn't name, because he'd never experienced it before. All he knew was that at that moment he thought Ana Ramsey was beautiful. He wanted to hold her against him, to absorb her confidence and be worthy of it.

"I meant it."

The atmosphere was hushed. A fly buzzed somewhere nearby, but otherwise everything was still. Sweat trickled down his face. Their bodies were taut as they tried to hold themselves separate. Still they inclined toward each other.

He rested his hand on the crown of her head and then gently brought it down to her neck. Her hair was soft against his callused palm. She tilted her head to one side and rested her cheek in his hand. He focused on her mouth. Her lips parted slightly even as he watched. They looked incredibly soft, solace-lending, pleasure-giving, vulnerable.

"Ana." He lowered his head. His lips touched hers.

"Ana!" another voice called.

They sprang apart. Trent's curse was vicious and as blistering as the white-hot Texas sun that beat down outside. Rana stepped away from him quickly and ran to the door of the greenhouse. Her heart was racing.

"Yes, Ruby? Here I am. What is it?"

"Telephone call for you, dear."

Rana glanced back at Trent. He shrugged and gave her a twisted smile, but it was strained with yearning. She crossed the yard at a trot and entered the house by the back door, which Ruby held open for her. "It's your mother."

Rana's footsteps faltered. "My mother?"

Ruby nodded, an unspoken question in her eyes. Ana Ramsey had no mother that she knew about.

Rana trudged up the stairs. She and her mother had conveyed messages to each other through Morey for the last six months. They hadn't spoken personally since Rana had walked out and thwarted Susan's plans for her daughter's marriage.

Why was Susan calling now? Rana wondered. Was she angry that Rana hadn't accepted the contract? Was she calling just to say hello? Was she calling to say, "I love you"?

Rana ridiculed herself for holding on to that hope. Nonetheless her hands were shaking and her voice trembled as she picked up the extension in her apartment and said, "Mother? Hello. How are you?"

"Morey is dead. I think the least you could do is return to New York for his funeral."

Six

*M*orey *is dead. Morey is dead.*

It was now almost thirty-six hours since Rana had first heard those words from her mother's lips, and she still couldn't believe them. After standing at the grave site and seeing his casket, the very idea still seemed too incredible to accept.

So much had happened since her mother had broken the news of Morey's death that it seemed as though the afternoon in the greenhouse with Trent had occurred in another lifetime. Both spiritual and physical fatigue settled on her as she reviewed the events subsequent to that phone call.

She had flung clothes haphazardly into a suitcase. Racing downstairs, she had asked Ruby if she could borrow her car. Ruby suggested that Trent could drive her to the airport, but Rana objected so strongly that Ruby gave her no further argument, even honoring her request that he not be called from the greenhouse to say good-bye. Rana told her friend that she would be away for an indefinite period of time. She didn't specify where she was going.

When the landlady expressed concern for Rana's obvious distress, the only explanation forthcoming was, "I'll tell you when I get back."

At Houston's Intercontinental Airport she had to watch two planes to New York take off without her before a standby seat on a third aircraft became available.

Once in New York, she took a cab to her apartment, where her mother was still living. They met face-to-face for the first time in six months. Susan was overtly hostile despite Rana's need to be consoled.

"You look ridiculous, Rana. I hope you don't expect me to claim you as mine, dressed like that."

"What about Morey, Mother?"

"He's dead." She held a gold Cartier lighter to the end of a cigarette, inhaled dramatically, and then blew a cloud of smoke over her head.

Rana, exhausted from the ordeal of getting to Houston from Galveston, waiting at the airport for hours, the long flight, not to mention her mental anguish, collapsed on the sofa and closed her eyes. It was now two o'clock in the morning in New York. Her spirit was trampled and her nerves were frayed, she had just lost her dearest friend and staunchest ally, and her mother's first comment had been about the way she looked. At that moment she hated Susan Ramsey.

"You told me that much on the telephone, Mother. What do you want me to do, beg you for the details?" She opened her eyes and confronted the woman she had never been able to please no matter how hard she had tried. "All right, I'm begging. What happened?" Her frustration finally got the best of her, and tears formed in her eyes.

Susan, with an almost smug expression, sat down on the far end of the long sofa. Despite the hour, she was immaculately groomed. Her satin robe was unwrinkled. "He died at home. One of his neighbors discovered the body late in the morning, when Morey didn't show up for a brunch date they had."

Morey lived alone; he and his wife had been divorced for years before Rana met him. He'd never gotten over the breakup of his marriage, but he could never give up gambling, either, which had been the crux of his marital problems.

"Was it a heart attack? A stroke?" Morey had been overweight, had high blood pressure, and smoked too much.

"Not exactly," Susan said coolly, scornfully. "Drugs were involved."

"Drugs!" Rana exclaimed, aghast. "I don't believe it."

"Not street drugs. Pills. Liquor. There was evidence in his apartment that he'd been drinking."

Rana's body seemed slowly to collapse, to fold in on itself like a house of cards. It *couldn't* be. She would never believe it. Suicide? No! "Was it an accident?" she asked hoarsely.

Susan ground out her cigarette in a crystal ashtray on the marble coffee table. "I think the police are ruling it an accidental death."

"But you think it was a suicide, don't you?"

"All I know is that when I last spoke with him, he was extremely upset over your turning down that marvelous contract. He was as shocked as I am that you would rather live like this," she said scathingly, waving her hand toward Rana as though she were filthy, "than like a princess. Morey was in financial trouble thanks to you."

Rana covered her face with her hands, but Susan persisted. "He had to move from those plush offices he had leased. When you so selfishly deserted both him and me, he went back to representing second-rate models and has-beens."

"Why didn't he tell me?" Rana groaned, asking the question of herself as much as of her mother.

Susan was all too happy to answer. "What good would it have done? If you had cared for anyone as much as you did yourself, you wouldn't have left in the first place. Why should you care what happened to some penny-ante agent— whom I wanted to discard years ago—if you don't care about your own mother?"

She lit another cigarette. Rana knew Susan wasn't finished yet, so she remained silent. It would serve no purpose to argue.

"I sacrificed everything to put you where you were, but you gave it all up without so much as a thank-you. You threw away a chance to marry one of the richest men in America. Does it matter to you that I can barely pay the bills on this place? No."

Susan could have found a more modest apartment that would still have been considered luxurious. She could have found herself a job. As Rana knew firsthand, her mother was certainly a capable manager. She was extremely attractive. Why didn't she find herself a well-to-do husband to henpeck? But Rana was too tired and upset to engage in a verbal battle with her mother by making any of those suggestions.

She pulled herself to her feet, weariness evident in every move. "I'm going to bed, Mother. When is the funeral?"

"Tomorrow at two. I've hired a limousine to pick us up. You'll find your retainer on the bedside table. Put it in. Your teeth are deplorable."

"You go in the limousine. I'll take a cab. Since I don't intend to wear that damned retainer another night of my life, and my teeth are deplorable, I'm sure you'll prefer riding in the limousine alone, rather than being seen with me."

At the funeral, Rana stood apart from the other mourners, hidden behind a pair of dark sunglasses and a black hat, which she had purchased at Macy's that morning. No one recognized her. No one looked at her. No one spoke to her as she stood weeping at the edge of the small crowd that dispersed as soon as the final prayer was said. Each one of its number seemed thankful that he had done his social duty and was now free to escape the heavy, muggy heat of the New Jersey cemetery and find relief in an air-conditioned car.

Rana lingered, even after Susan swept past her without a nod. *Why, Morey, why?* she asked the carnation-blanketed casket. Why hadn't he told her he was in financial trouble? Had he taken his own life?

It was too horrible a thought to contemplate, but she couldn't help remembering the excitement she had heard in his voice when he'd told her of the substantial contract, the despondency he had conveyed when he'd asked her to reconsider the offer.

And now, driving from the Houston airport back to Galveston, those questions were still haunting Rana. To add to her misery, rain was pelting the highway. It was a dark, ponderous, dismal rain that matched her mood perfectly.

Her future stretched out in front of her like the flat coastal highway. Unrelieved. Monotonous. Dreary. She could see no light in that future. How could she ever be happy and carefree with the indelible stain of Morey's suicide on her conscience?

The house was dark. She noticed that Trent's car was gone. He and Ruby must have gone out together. Picking up her suitcase, she ran through the driving rain to the back door.

Leaving her suitcase on the sleeping porch, she took off her hat and shook the rain from it. She slipped out of her jacket and spread it over a chair to dry. Her shoes came off next, and with them her stockings.

Barefoot, she padded into the kitchen. It was uncharacteristically gloomy. Even the crisply starched ruffled curtains at the windows looked sad and limp against the bleak landscape beyond them. She got a drink of tepid water from the tap in the sink, but after taking two swallows, she left the glass on the drainboard. She was so disconsolate that every movement was a chore. Her limbs felt leaden, and it took a supreme effort to move them. Blackest depression weighed her down.

She had been a baby when her father had died, so she didn't remember. Now, for the first time in her life, she had suffered the death of someone she really cared about. How did anyone survive the loss of a beloved spouse, a child? The finality of death was dreadful.

Without turning on any lights, she went through the shadowed dining room into the central hall. Rain trickled down the tall, narrow windows on either side of the front door. It looked mournful, silvery, cold. It looked like tears. Rana stared up the dark staircase and wondered where she would get the energy to climb those steps to her room.

Listlessly, she dropped onto the deacon's bench beneath the stairs. Propping her elbows on her knees, she laid her head in her hands and began to cry. She had wept quietly, politely, at the funeral, but she hadn't lifted the floodgate of her grief.

Now tears, scalding and bitter, fell from her eyes with

the same incessant pattern as the rain falling outside. They ran down her cheeks and into her mouth. They dripped from her chin. Her shoulders shook with racking sobs.

She sensed he was there only a second before she felt his hand on her shoulder. She raised her head. He was standing in front of her, looming as tall as a pillar. The gray light was dim in the hallway, particularly beneath the stairs. She could barely distinguish his features, but she could tell that his dark brows were drawn together with worry.

Her mother had offered her no words of consolation. Rana had been a stranger to the others attending the funeral. She needed comfort, craved some token of reassurance. She reached toward the only available source. Mindlessly, she clutched his arms.

Instantly responsive, Trent sat down on the hard deacon's bench beside her and wrapped his arms around her. He said nothing, only pressed his face against her damp hair. He cupped the back of her head and forced her face down into the hollow between his shoulder and neck. She burrowed there, letting the soft cloth of his shirt absorb the torrent of relentless, salty tears.

His fingers stirred in her hair, and he was amazed to find it so thick and lush, and so soft to his touch. When his fingers settled on her scalp, he massaged it tenderly. His lips touched her ear.

"I've been so worried about you."

As though grasping his concern as something rare and precious, Rana's fingers curled into the front of his shirt.

Through it she could feel the warmth of his skin, the shape of his hard muscles, the crinkly texture of his chest hair.

"Where did you go, Ana?"

The pseudonym was foreign to her, and for a moment she couldn't imagine why he was calling her by the wrong name. Then she remembered. The name was a lie. It was as phony as the rest of her. Her whole life had been a string of fakeries, a tapestry of superficiality. At that moment she longed for nothing more than to hear her name, Rana, from Trent's lips. She wanted to feel his breath as he spoke her name against her ear. She wanted to see her name forming on his lips.

"Why are you crying? Where have you been?"

"Don't ask me, Trent."

"I find you crying alone in the dark. How can you expect me to ignore that? Tell me what's wrong. Can I help? Where have you been and why did you go without saying good-bye to me?"

She pushed herself away from him and sniffed. Unabashedly she wiped her face with the backs of her hands. Suddenly she realized she wasn't wearing her glasses. But he wouldn't recognize her tear-bloated eyes in the darkness.

"I had to go out of town to a friend's funeral."

He waited a moment, then laid his arm across her shoulders. He ran the back of his index finger down her cheek, picking up tears that her fists had left behind. "I'm sorry. Was it a close friend?"

"Very."

"A sudden death?"

She covered her face with her hands again. "Yes, yes." She moaned. "A suicide."

Trent hissed a curse, and the hand resting on her shoulder tensed. He tucked her head beneath his chin again. "That's tough. I know. Before I played for the Mustangs, I had a buddy on another team. His knees got so banged up, they finally told him he couldn't play ball anymore. He shot himself. I know just how you feel."

"No, you don't," she cried angrily, shoving herself out of his arms and standing abruptly. "You weren't to blame for your friend's death." She tried to make it to the stairs, but he caught up with her and, grabbing her arm, spun her around.

"Are you saying you were to blame for this suicide?"

"Yes."

"I don't believe that," he said firmly, shaking her slightly. "You can't take responsibility for someone else's life. No one can."

"Oh, Trent, tell me that until I believe it." Her hands folded around his steely biceps, and she gazed up at him imploringly. "Repeat it a thousand times if that's what it takes to convince me."

He wrapped his arms around her and drew her close, holding her against him tightly. "It's true. Believe me. If this friend was inclined toward self-destruction, there was little you could have done except possibly delay it."

"I let him down when he needed me."

"Most people learn to cope with disappointments. You're not to blame that your friend didn't."

He closed his arms around her and held her for a long time, rocking her slightly back and forth. "Better now?" he asked softly.

"Yes. The hurt is still there, but it isn't so sharp."

He had turned them so that her back was to the wall. She leaned against it, but left her arms resting lightly on Trent's shoulders. He pressed his lips to her neck.

"I'm only sorry that you had to suffer over this."

Unconsciously she let her head tip backward. "Thank you. I haven't been able to talk to anyone about it. I needed this . . . needed you."

"Then I'm glad I was here."

His caresses had gone beyond consolation and were now of another nature entirely. "So am I."

"Ana?"

"Hm?"

He gazed down at her, his expression filled with wonder. "Ana?"

Then his mouth was on hers, hot and hard and urgent. Imprisoning her face between his hands, he slanted his lips across hers. He made a low, growling, hungry sound deep in his throat.

Rana's hands clenched on his shoulders, taking up handfuls of fabric. She turned her head away and gasped, "No."

"Yes."

He gave her no other chance to protest. His mouth was commanding as it trapped hers in a kiss that robbed her of will.

Her body went weak, and she would have slumped against the wall, had his hard form not been pressed against her, holding her up.

Her arms folded around his neck. She answered the low mating sounds that emanated from his chest with murmurs of want—primal, untamed, untutored want.

His tongue slipped inside her mouth, and it was as though her mind exploded in a riot of color and light. The warm, damp, velvety-rough texture of his tongue was new and delicious to her. She allowed it the liberties it seemed to take as its due. Its searching thrusts elicited thrilling sensations throughout her body. Her breasts tingled. Behind them, her heart was thudding with the deep bass pounding of a timpani.

They paused to breathe, looked at each other with astonishment, then fell on each other again. Having had that first taste, they were hungrier than ever, and ate at each other's mouths.

Trent was the aggressor, but Rana was more than compliant. Hers was a greediness stemming from ignorance and deprivation. Her young husband had never kissed her with this kind of unbridled desire. Other men wouldn't have dared.

Trent knew no such restriction. His mouth twisted over hers repeatedly. He couldn't get enough of kissing her. And soon kissing wasn't enough.

His hands slid down her arms to her waist. With a quick, savage motion, he yanked her up against him and ground his front against the cleft between her thighs.

"I want you," he growled as his mouth traced a fiery path down the column of her neck.

"We can't."

"We *will.*"

"Where's Ruby?"

"We're alone."

"But—"

"No arguments. You and I both knew this was destined to happen."

And she had known. From the moment she had stepped out of her room and seen him in the hallway, she had known that Trent Gamblin posed a threat to her. Not a sinister threat, but a threat nonetheless. She had known in that instant, when she first looked into his chocolate-colored eyes and fell victim to his charming smile, that he would change her life. Now she resigned herself to that fate . . . but resignation had little to do with her acquiescence when he laid his hands on her breasts. Her eyes closed as he massaged her nipples gently, rubbing in slow circles, dragging his thumbs back and forth across them until he got the reaction he wanted. Even then, he continued the love play as he nestled his face in her neck and let his mouth coast back and forth over her fragrant, warm skin.

He unbuttoned her blouse with frantic clumsiness, eager to see what his hands had discovered. He had known she wasn't wearing a bra, but he was pleasantly surprised by the lacy sheerness of her slip.

"My God," he breathed as he stepped back to look at what he had uncovered. He wished for a light, because what he imagined he saw were incredibly beautiful breasts, not large, but full and well shaped. They filled the cups of the slip with skin that looked creamy enough to drink and nipples as sweet and lovely as baby rosebuds.

With his fingertips barely touching the lace, he caressed her, this dream woman who lived inside the ugly clothes. Except she was real. This wasn't another of the fantasies he had had to rely on to put him to sleep lately. This was actually happening. He was touching her.

Through the lace her skin was warm. And when he lightly stroked the delicious-looking crests, they responded in a way that made his sex surge to ready hardness. He actually groaned with the force of his longing. He peeled down the straps of her slip and, with a sound that was part sigh, part moan, took one tight peak into his mouth.

Rana cried his name and buried her fingers in the thick mass of his hair. She bent her head over his, squeezing her eyes closed. Her breath came out in rapid little pants that had a way of getting trapped in her throat. Each sweet tugging motion of his mouth coaxed a responding contraction from her womb. She grew moist with need.

As though her body had silently telegraphed that need, his hands reached for the hem of her skirt and raised it. When she felt his hands on her thighs, she shuddered. His callused palms created an exciting friction against the smooth length of her thighs. She held her breath in expectation. Surely he wouldn't. Not here. Not now.

But Trent was driven to discover. And then to know, and know thoroughly.

His hands smoothed all the way up her thighs, enjoying every silky inch. They settled on her hips. He pressed his thumbs against her hipbones and rotated them slowly, mesmerizingly, while his fingers bit deep into her derriere.

Then his thumbs met at her navel and traveled down over the satin smoothness of her panties, disappearing into the V of her femininity.

Rana gasped. Her hands gripped his shoulders out of fear of falling, or of flying out of the universe. She no longer felt earthbound. Gravity had no power over her like the touch of Trent's hands.

Her breath shuddered in and out when he slipped his hands beneath the waistband of her panties and eased them down. Bravely she opened her eyes and met his. They were hot. Even in the darkness, she could see them burning. It never occurred to her to protest. She didn't want to. Her body was yearning for his possession.

She stepped out of her panties with a remarkable lack of awkwardness. His mouth rewarded her with another searing kiss. His tongue was intent. Each stroking caress was executed with full concentration.

His mouth moved down her neck, leaving hot, random kisses in its wake. Her heart soared when his lips fastened onto her breast again. He caressed the nipple with lazy circles and airy brushes of his tongue.

She sobbed.

He touched her.

She enveloped his fingers in honeyed heat.

He caressed, slowly and gently, creating never-ending spirals of pleasure.

She felt her body quicken.

With his fingertips he coaxed her to surrender.

She did.

Wave after wave of blissful sensation cascaded over her. She trembled with each fiery inundation. They seemed to go on forever. When the last one finally receded like the lacy benediction of a wave against the shore, where sparkling bubbles burst and were absorbed into the sand one by one, she wanted to leave her eyes closed and sleep forever.

But she felt his breath against her cheek as he kissed it gently. She opened her eyes. Trent was staring down at her with a tender smile curving his beautiful mouth.

But his body wasn't as serene as his face. She could feel the tension of passion as yet unleashed. He worked his hand between their bodies and opened his jeans.

His hands cupped her bottom. He lifted her up and spread her thighs over his lap until she was straddling it. He slipped inside her, and her head fell forward onto his shoulder as they sighed their mutual gratification.

He was so warm, so smooth, so hard. The petals of her body closed around him. He moaned his supreme pleasure. And it was the dearest sound she had ever heard. She had pleased someone and it had nothing to do with how she looked.

He reached high, and she gloried in the strength and power of his possession. Her soft whimpers told him so. For her, he wanted to be better than he'd ever been. He kissed her breasts lingeringly, lovingly.

Rana didn't think it was possible, but she felt new stirrings of desire deep within her. With each searching motion of his body, the desire escalated, until she was racing toward the precipice of reason again.

He waited, baring his teeth with the effort to hold back. Only when her crisis came did he relax his control. Then he experienced a release so complete, so wondrous that it shook not only his body, but his heart and soul as well.

Damply, weakly, they clung to each other. Their hearts beat in time. His breath fanned her shoulder where he rested his head. Hers soughed against his throat.

The rain tapping at the windows was like background music now. The ticking of the clock on the mantel in the parlor could be heard faintly over their harsh breathing and the pounding of their hearts.

At last he set her down. Then he pulled her close and hugged her tight. He was amazed that she was so slight. His arms encompassed her with room to spare. He planted a tender kiss on the crown of her head.

Wordlessly taking her hand, he led her toward the stairs. He went ahead, but kept his eyes on her as they made the long, slow climb to the second story. He pulled her inside his bedroom and pushed the door closed, shutting the world out. Leaving her to stand in the middle of the room, he went to the bed and turned it down. Then he extended his hand to her and nodded toward the bed.

"We have to talk," she said huskily.

"No, we don't."

Slowly he began unbuttoning his shirt. Rana's breasts ached with reawakening desire. He peeled the shirt off and tossed it heedlessly onto the floor. Hooking his thumbs in the waistband of his jeans, he pulled them down.

When he straightened up, he was naked. And splendid. He came swaggering toward her across the shadowy room. The watery light from the windows cast beguiling, fluid shadows over his nakedness. She wanted him again.

Her arms dangled loosely at her sides, a testimony to her compliance. Without a word he pulled her unbuttoned blouse from the waistband of her skirt. It joined his shirt on the floor. He eased the straps of her slip down her arms and lowered it as far as her waist. His hands made one tender pass across her breasts. He dipped his head and touched the crest of one with his tongue; then, because it performed with such feminine beauty, he dallied there longer than he had planned.

"Trent," she gasped when she felt her knees about to buckle beneath her.

"Shhh."

He unbuttoned her skirt with dispatch and pulled it and the slip down to the floor. They faced each other naked. He swept her up in his arms and deposited her lovingly on the bed, then followed her down, covering her.

She welcomed his weight. It pressed her into the mattress, and she loved the feeling. He was hard and heavy. She ran her hands down the supple expanse of his back and over his buttocks. She'd never had access to a man like this before. His sheer masculinity was a curiosity she wanted to explore and examine. Playfully she dug her short nails into his buttocks, and he grinned.

She kissed him. Wantonly.

He kissed her. Wetly.

He slid his tongue in and out of her mouth until she was breathless. "Still want to talk?" he drawled as his parted lips meandered over her neck and chest.

"We should." She moaned when he covered her nipple with his mouth, rubbed it with his tongue.

"You've never learned to relax, Miss Ramsey."

He moved lower, kissing her stomach as he went. She shivered with carnal delight. His tongue dipped into her navel, laved it thoroughly.

"Trent?"

"Hm?"

Instinctively she drew her knees up. He positioned himself between them.

"We really should—"

His next caress was so giving, so unselfish, it stopped her words . . . her heart.

"This is what we should be doing," he whispered against her softness. "And I intend to go on doing it for a long, long time."

Seven

You never did tell me where Ruby is."

He shifted his long legs beneath the sheets and found a warmer spot next to hers. "You didn't ask." He butted his nose against her jaw.

"I did so."

"You did? I must have had my mind on something else."

"All you said was that we were alone."

"Good thing, too." He chuckled before his mouth settled on hers for a deep, satisfying kiss. "I'm sure that hallway has never seen such excitement."

She yanked on a chest hair, and he yelped. They laughed together, and when their laughter subsided he said, "Auntie left this morning to sit with a sick friend. She said she might not return until tomorrow. So," he said, dragging out the word, "tonight we have the whole house to ourselves."

"But we're not using the whole house, only this bed."

"That's the general idea."

Their lips met. The kiss was soft and sweet. His lips plucked at hers, and they responded. "I never imagined that I'd be with you this way," she whispered against his mouth.

"I imagined it. A lot."

"Well, actually I *did* imagine it. I just . . . Oh, you know what I mean."

"I couldn't imagine you *this* way." He ran his hands over her hips caressingly.

"What do you mean?"

"I couldn't imagine what your body was like beneath your clothes. I confess that one of my better-developed talents is being able to undress a woman with my eyes." He frowned. "I couldn't even begin to undress you, and it drove me nuts. I wanted to know what you were like naked." His hands moved to her breasts and kneaded them lovingly. "I am delightfully surprised."

Moving lower, he began loving her breasts with his mouth. Rana laid her hands on either side of his head. His hard jaw was getting bristly from his beard. It rasped pleasantly against her skin.

The rain continued through the night, and so did their lovemaking. Surely no two human beings had ever been more physically compatible. His slightest touch awakened a vibrant sexuality that she hadn't known she possessed. They made love repeatedly. The mood and tempo varied, but his body never failed to bring hers to a pinnacle of sensation and satisfaction.

Gradually she was overcoming her shyness with him. At first she had been hesitant to initiate anything, even to touch him.

"Lay your hands on my chest," he urged breathlessly when he surprised her by rolling her atop him. "Touch me. Please touch me."

She did as he asked, though her touch was tentative. Then she felt the beating of his heart against her palm and she allowed herself to do what she had wanted to do many times. Her hands thoroughly explored his chest. Her fingers combed through the dense hair and investigated the nipples until he was gasping and writhing beneath her.

She could feel him, full and hard, against her middle, and she wanted to know him in the most intimate way. Moving aside, she knelt over him and touched him with her mouth. Trent uttered a hoarse cry. He wound handfuls of her hair around his fists. Her lips and tongue tested his strength delicately, until he could bear no more, and positioned her over him again.

And just when Rana thought there was no more to learn, he would introduce her to an entirely new erotic experience.

Only once during the night were they out of harmony with each other, and that was when he reached for the lamp on the bedside table.

"No!" She reacted violently, and drew the sheet up over herself.

His amazement showed. "But I want to see you," he explained tenderly. "I want to see us together."

"No, please, Trent. If you want me to stay, leave the light off."

"I don't understand." He didn't. Up until that moment, she had demonstrated a willingness for them to express their mutual feelings in any way. Why the aversion to having the light on? He took her in his arms. "You're beautiful. I can feel how beautiful you are. Let me see you."

She snuggled her face against his chest, loving the way its forest of hair felt against her cheeks and lips. "Please, Trent. I like it better dark. Please."

She knew that her hair was tousled, wild, and abandoned, the way it had often been photographed. Her glasses were still downstairs in her purse. And though she had gained some weight, her body would look much as it did in print ads and commercials, because cameras added pounds.

Tonight was so special. He was loving her without any thought of her appearance. She didn't want to spoil it by risking discovery now.

Regretfully Trent consented. Later he even found her aversion to having the light on amusing. "I didn't realize you were so bashful."

Rana knew he wouldn't think so if he'd ever been behind the scenes at a fashion show. The haughty models strutted down the runways looking cool, confident, and unruffled, while backstage, pandemonium reigned. She had often been stripped even as she switched hats and earrings.

Other hands had dressed and undressed her as many times as she had herself. One couldn't be self-conscious about nakedness and work with designers, seamstresses, and photographers. Their touches were so impersonal, soon she had ceased to be aware of them. Her mother had never been one to show any affection.

Perhaps that was why Rana had responded so urgently and rapidly to Trent's touch, she thought. Oh, yes, she must be starved for the loving touch of another human being. If he wanted to think her bashful, she would let him.

"Does it surprise you that I'm so shy?"

"Frankly, yes. Especially since you've been married." He strummed her back for a few moments, then asked, "Can you tell me about that or is it too painful a subject?"

"It was, but it ended so long ago that sometimes I think it happened to someone else. I was fresh out of high school."

"He was your high-school sweetheart?"

"Something like that."

Actually, they had dated only several months before they got married. Patrick, like most young men, had been dazzled by her. But she had managed to break through the barrier of his awe, and she and Patrick had fallen into an idealistic, immature kind of love.

Susan was already talking about a move to New York and planning how to coordinate Rana's career with a few years of college. Rana resisted. She wanted a career, because she loved beautiful clothes and couldn't imagine anything better than getting paid for modeling them. But she didn't want a career orchestrated by her mother, a career that would exclude everything else, especially Patrick.

So she had talked him into a whirlwind marriage. It was a desperate attempt on Rana's part to escape her mother's clutches. When Susan heard their plans, she had been furious. But she was a relentless, cunning fighter. Instead of refusing to let them marry, she permitted it.

From the outset, she smothered the young couple, advising on this, arranging that, until Patrick felt useless and emasculated. The final blow to his ego came when Susan intervened with the personnel manager at a company where he had applied for employment.

Rana, admitting to herself that she had used him abominably, and knowing how unhappy their marriage was making him, had offered him a way out. He readily took it.

Six months after the wedding, the marriage ended in divorce. Rana and her mother moved to New York as soon as arrangements could be made. In the long run Susan got exactly what she wanted.

"He was very sweet," Rana told Trent now. "Good and kind to me. But it was doomed from the beginning."

"Why?"

"My mother was constantly butting in, and my husband wanted to live his own life."

"Your mother? You've never mentioned any living relatives."

"We're not very close. Not any longer."

"Are you close to anyone, Ana?" he asked, his tone of voice soft.

The conversation was getting too personal, and she didn't want that. She looked up at him with a mischievous smile and tiptoed her fingers down his front. "Right now, I'm very close to you."

He grunted with pleasure and lowered his mouth to hers.

Later, as she dozed, he went downstairs and made scrambled eggs and bacon. He carried the meal up on a tray. If the rattling dishes hadn't awakened her, the tantalizing aromas would have. She sat up, blinking sleep from her eyes.

"Hungry?" he asked with a grin when he saw that she was awake.

"Starving, though I didn't realize it until now."

He set the tray on the bed and tossed her one of his shirts. "May I turn the light on now?" he asked after she slipped the shirt on and modestly closed a few of the buttons.

She reached for her purse, which he had had the foresight to bring up along with her panties, and took out the tinted glasses. "Yes," she answered, putting them on.

"Do you have to?" he asked, nodding toward the glasses.

"Do you want me to dribble orange juice all over your bed?"

He winked. "That might be kinda kinky."

She let his remark pass as a joke and was glad that he didn't pursue the topic of the glasses. Eagerly they attacked the food.

"You know, don't you, that you had me ranting and raving?" he said, biting into a last piece of toast.

She set her coffee cup back in its saucer and moved the tray aside. She had cleaned her plate and was now reclining against the pillows he had piled behind her.

"Over what?"

"Over your sudden disappearance. I nearly went crazy worrying about you."

"I'm sorry I didn't say good-bye. There wasn't time."

"Was that the only reason you didn't see me before you left?"

"What other reason could there be?"

"Things were getting pretty hot in the greenhouse. And I don't mean that in meteorological terms." He took her hand and rubbed his thumb over the ridge of her knuckles. "If Ruby hadn't called you to the phone, I think I would have taken you right there in the dirt. Love among the blooms. Hothouse romance." He was teasing, but he grew serious when he asked, "Were you running from something you couldn't handle, Ana? From me?"

"Possibly. I don't know. In any event, you caught me, didn't you?"

"You needed to be caught, Miss Ramsey."

"*Needed* to be?" She cocked her head to one side.

"Uh-huh," he said, leaning back and propping himself up on his elbows, not realizing how complacent he looked. He had pulled on a pair of shorts when he went downstairs, but they only emphasized his sex. Right then he epitomized male smugness. "I think you've needed a man for a long time, someone to scratch that itch you had, someone to satisfy your dark, secret desires."

"And you filled the bill?" she asked carefully.

By way of an answer, he shrugged. That self-satisfied expression on his face said it all.

Rana sprang off the bed so quickly that he didn't have time to react until she was out the door and halfway across the hall. "What's the matter? Where are you going?"

She spun around and confronted him, enraged. "I don't *need* anybody, Mr. Gamblin. Especially a man who makes love to me out of a sense of pity!"

"Pity! What the hell are you talking about?"

"Figure it out." She stamped into her room and slammed the door, locking it quickly. The thought that his lovemaking had been a charitable act wasn't to be borne. She had come home feeling lonely and desperate. He had lent her comfort and she had grasped at it. Had his loving been no more than a means of rejuvenating poor Miss Ramsey, lifting her out of the depths of despair?

He rattled the door angrily and banged against it with his fists. "Open this door."

"Go away."

"I'm warning you."

"I said to go away!"

"If you don't open this door, I'll tear it down, and you'll have to tell Ruby how it happened."

"Your threats of brute force don't frighten me."

Perhaps they should have. The next sound she heard was the crashing of the door against the wall as he shoved it open. Instinctively she cowered, crossing her arms over her chest. He grabbed her by the shoulders, jerked her up so that her toes were barely touching the floor, and shook her.

"You're the most stubborn woman I've ever known. Pity!" he scoffed. "Darling, no one carries pity *that* far. Don't you know love when you see it?"

She had been holding herself rigid. Now she went limp in his arms. "Love?" she repeated weakly.

"Yes, love," he said, bobbing his head. "Ever heard of it? I love you, and you know what? It scares the hell out of me. I've never been so gut-twisted in all my life. You've rung my chimes worse than any linebacker ever did. I haven't known whether I was coming or going. I've never felt like this, been this much out of control. I've never been more miserable or felt so damn good. It's terrible."

He demonstrated just how terrible it was by sealing her surprised mouth with his. Walking her backward, he maneuvered them to the sofa. Still holding her against him, he fell onto it. His hands had no regard for his own shirt. He tore it open, freeing her breasts for the wild caresses of his mouth. Just as frantically, he rid himself of his shorts.

Their union was swift. He secured himself deep inside her. Only then did he become still, while the heat within him simmered. His lips flirted with her ear, and he rasped, "In case I haven't yet made myself clear, I love you. Here's how much." He began to move.

She enfolded him with her limbs, with her heart. When the tumult came, it was explosive. They didn't recover from it for a long time.

Rana closed her eyes and let the shower's spray pound over her body. She washed carefully, lathering more lavishly than usual and sliding her hands over her body with an appreciation for it she had never had before. She was acutely aware of each sensation. What did her skin feel like to Trent? She tried to imagine, smiling as she recalled every adoring word he had whispered as he loved her.

He had been disappointed when, after a nap on her couch, she had suggested that he return to his own room.

"Why?" he had asked, snuggling closer. "I like it here. And here. And here." With caressing hands he indicated all the parts of her body he loved.

She swatted his hands away before they got the best of her common sense. "Ruby might come back at any time. What if she checks up on us and finds us together?"

"What if she does? I'm a big boy."

"Hm, I'll say." She sighed, caressing him.

His sigh turned into a groan of arousal. "Darlin', that's not a very good way of talking me into leaving. Or did you change your mind?" He eased her onto her back as his mouth reached for hers.

"No, I didn't change my mind." She shoved him away, and he had to jump to his feet or lose his balance and roll off the couch.

"How about a quick shower?" he suggested as she pushed him toward the door.

"How about a long one?"

"You mean it?" he said, his face lighting up.

"Alone."

"Oh." His smile collapsed. "Do you want to jog first?"

"You go ahead without me. I don't have the energy."

That brought his smile back. "I feel like I could climb Mount Everest or take on all the Pittsburgh Steelers or slay a dragon." He kissed her hard and swiftly before leaving.

Now, stepping from the shower, Rana played that scene again in her head, as she had recalled every precious second of the night since he had first taken her in his arms. She went over every word, every touch. She relished them, treasuring them, because she had never known a love like this.

And why not admit it? She *was* in love with Trent Gamblin.

She gazed at herself in the foggy bathroom mirror, wondering if the evidence of that newfound love was shining in her eyes. Those exotic eyes she took such pains to hide stared back at her, limpid with emotion. What would Trent think if she allowed him to see them? Would he think they were as mysterious and lovely as they were touted to be? Would he think they were beautiful?

She opened the cabinet and took out a brown eye crayon. She turned it over and over in her hand, the way a former smoker handles a forbidden cigarette. A stroke of the crayon here, a dab there, a smudged line underneath the lower lashes. Should she? Just a subtle highlight to enhance the almond shape of her eyes? A whisk of cheek color in the hollow beneath her cheekbones? A little lip gloss?

She thought wistfully of all the white clothes left behind in New York. Their color made her olive complexion and dark red hair breathtaking by contrast. Cinched waistbands, provocative necklines, flowing skirts, and tailored slacks made the most of her figure. For just a moment she yearned to be as beautiful as she possibly could be.

What would Trent think of his lover then?

"You can't really love me," she had whispered in the aftermath of their passion.

"I do."

"I know what kind of woman you're usually with. I'm not that type."

"Maybe that's why I love you so much. I've dated many

beautiful women, but they're so damn shallow compared to you. You have substance. A soul. I love your body. I love what it does to mine. But I fell in love with what you are on the inside. You're not just a pretty shell. You're a complete woman."

Rana returned the eye crayon to the shelf in the cabinet and closed the door firmly. She covered her face with her hands and breathed deeply. Feminine vanity tempted her to be beautiful for him. But would he still love her if he knew she had been exactly the kind of woman he now scorned?

She wasn't under any illusions about their future. They had none. There wouldn't be a happy ending. In only a short time he would be leaving for training camp. When he left, she would lose him forever.

But *now*, while she was with him, she would bask in his professions of love. There had been so few satisfying emotional relationships in her life. Her mother didn't really know what love was. Morey had loved her, but for some reason he hadn't felt that he could confide in her.

Every time she thought of his death, she was devastated all over again. Had he taken his own life? The possibility plagued her, but Trent's loving had soothed even that deep wound.

Their time together was destined to be fleeting. But she would live every minute of it without regret. She would be Ana Ramsey, because that was what he needed right now.

She had barely pulled on a pair of sloppy jeans and an oversized blue chambray shirt when he knocked on her door. "Open up."

"Coming. Please don't come crashing in again." When she opened the door to him, she asked, "Are you going to repair the lock before Ruby sees it?"

"Are you going to give me a kiss?"

"You're drenched with sweat!"

"My lips aren't." She leaned toward him and touched only his puckered lips with hers. "Guess that'll have to do for now," he said grudgingly.

She laughed. "Are you hungry?"

"We had breakfast at four A.M. In a case like that, what does one eat at nine?"

"How about grilled-ham-and-cheese sandwiches?"

"Sounds great."

"I'll start them. You go shower, please," she said, waving her hand in front of her nose.

Ten minutes later he joined her in the kitchen. "You certainly smell better," she said laughingly. "I sliced up some fruit for a salad and—"

He stopped her speech by hauling her toward him, encircling her with his arms, and planting a damp, hot kiss on her mouth. He touched her slightly crooked teeth with his tongue. "I love the way you taste." His mouth slid down her throat. "All of you," he mumbled into her cleavage. His mouth returned to hers and his tongue delved deep.

"Your sandwich is getting cold," she murmured drowsily when they came up for air.

"And I'm getting hot." He nuzzled her middle with his.

Rana cleared her throat and stepped out of his embrace. "You're shameless. Now, sit down and eat."

"You're getting as bossy as Aunt Ruby."

They ate their brunch, but went about it slowly, because they often lapsed into staring spells. He mentioned her glasses again and asked if she would take them off. "Then I couldn't see you," she explained, and diverted him by pecking a string of kisses along his jaw and finally finding his mouth.

"Hello, dears, anybody home?" Ruby called from the entrance hall.

They broke apart. Rana looked dismayed, and her cheeks filled with rosy color. Trent, looking like the cat who got the cream, smiled at her lazily. "In here, Aunt Ruby. I was just eating something delicious."

Rana glared at him as Ruby came bustling through the door. "What's that, dear? Oh, how lovely! Miss Ramsey's feeding you."

"Uh-huh."

Rana jumped from her seat and pulled out a chair for Ruby. "Join us, please. Is your friend doing well?"

"Yes, yes, much better. Wanted some company, more than anything. But tell me, how was your trip? When did you get back?"

Rana filled Ruby in on the essential facts surrounding

her trip, leaving out the details. "I apologize for leaving in such a hurry without any explanation."

"Under the circumstances, I understand," Ruby said, laying a sympathetic hand on the younger woman's arm. "Did Trent tell you he had your car repaired while you were away?"

"No," he answered for her. "We've seen a lot of each other since she got back, but we never got around to discussing cars."

Rana shot him another fulminating look, but luckily Ruby was too distracted to notice his double entendre. "Would you like me to fix you a sandwich, Ruby?" Rana asked. "I haven't put away the makings yet, and you look tired."

"Thank you, dear, maybe I will let you make me a sandwich. If neither of you needs me this afternoon, I think I'll stay in my room and nap. My friend and I talked into the wee hours of the morning. The poor thing has no one to talk with. The children rarely visit."

Rana prepared and grilled another sandwich. Trent nibbled on sliced cantaloupe and watermelon. His eyes rarely left Rana. They transmitted smoky looks full of implication.

"That was delicious," Ruby told Rana when she had finished eating. "Is there anything either of you needs?"

"No, Auntie," Trent said, solicitously helping his aunt from her chair. "You go rest. Miss Ramsey and I are perfectly capable of taking care of ourselves. And why not let me take you out to dinner tonight?"

Ruby patted his cheek affectionately. "Isn't he a dear boy?"

"Yes, he is," Rana said with a happy smile.

"Did you mean that?" Trent asked Rana a few minutes later, after Ruby had retired to her room down the hall and they were alone.

"What?" She was rinsing out dishes at the sink. It had taken some convincing, but Ruby had finally consented to let her do the chore.

"About my being a dear boy?" He slid his arms around her from behind. Immediately his hands found her breasts and began to massage them. "Why do you hide these behind such bulky clothes? You've got beautiful, enticing breasts. Don't you have something clingy to wear?"

She tried to struggle free, but she didn't try very hard. "No, I like loose clothes. What difference does it make to you?"

"Because I'd like to look at them." His thumbs drifted back and forth across her nipples until they became erect. "See what I mean? I hate to miss seeing that."

"Stop it, Trent. Ruby might come in."

"She's sleeping," he whispered against the back of her neck. "Wanna go play in the greenhouse?"

"The greenhouse?" A delicious lassitude was seeping through her, robbing her of the strength to protest.

"Yeah. I could go for some hot, steamy sex with you right now."

"You're shameless."

"I'm horny," he whispered, turning her around to face him.

"Still?"

"Grilled-ham-and-cheese sandwiches always have that effect on me." She linked her arms around his neck. "Especially when a lusty broad like you has cooked them for me." His arms went around her waist. He slid his hands into the back pockets of her jeans and drew her against him. "You have the cutest little butt." He squeezed it as he fitted himself against her.

The kiss started out passionate and only got deeper. Their mouths opened to each other; tongues met. Anchoring her hips against the side of the counter with the firm pressure of his, he unbuttoned her blouse far enough to get a hand inside. He cupped her breast lovingly, gently squeezed it, and lightly rolled the nipple between his fingers.

"I want you," he said roughly. "The greenhouse or the bedroom?"

"Trent, we can't," she said feebly.

"How come?"

"It's the middle of the day."

"So?"

"I really need to paint. I've got work to do. Four new orders."

"Okay," he said with a heavy sigh. "I'll leave you alone to work if you'll let me stay in your apartment while I study my playbook."

She watched his face carefully, looking for signs of trickery. "All right," she conceded at last. "But you've got to promise to behave."

"I promise."

They went upstairs to her apartment. They even made a concerted effort to stick to their resolutions. But as it turned out, they made slow, lazy, afternoon love.

It was wonderful, but Trent was faintly disappointed that Ana insisted on closing the heavy drapes and blocking out most of the light. He wanted to see sunlight pouring over her body. Lying beside her on the bed, he watched her drowsing in the contented aftermath of desire. He wondered how he ever could have thought she was plain.

She was beautiful. She wasn't like any other woman he'd ever met. She filled an emptiness in his life he hadn't even known was there. And now that he had found her, he wasn't about to let her go.

Eight

O
h, here she is now."

Rana heard Trent's voice the moment she stepped through the front door, and, following it, the familiar tread of his feet on the hardwood floors.

"Ana?"

"Hi."

He rounded the corner connecting the center hall to the parlor and took her in his arms for a swift kiss. "There's someone here I want you to meet."

"But—"

"You've heard of Tom Tandy, wide receiver for the Mustangs. He's got the best hands in the NFL. He drove down for a visit. I've been telling him all about you."

She tried to dig her heels in, but Trent was pushing her toward the front parlor. She didn't want to meet anyone, in her frazzled condition. She had been shopping for supplies and she felt hot and disheveled.

And then there was always the chance that she might be recognized when she was introduced to someone. She and Trent had been together for some time. His affection was genuine. Of that she was certain. More than ever she dreaded his finding out that she wasn't exactly who she pretended to be. How he would feel if ever he discovered her true identity, she couldn't guess, but she didn't want to risk it. Everything had been so idyllic, spoiling it now was unthinkable.

They hadn't been able to keep their love affair a secret from Ruby. That first evening, when Trent had held true to his promise to take them out to dinner, Ruby had shrewdly assessed the situation.

From behind her menu she had said, "It took the two of you long enough to discover each other."

"What do you mean, Aunt Ruby?" Trent asked innocently.

Ruby lowered the corner of the menu and gave him a baleful look. "I'm not senile or undersexed, young man, and I resent your implication that I don't know about these things. Where do you think *I* was last night?"

"You said you were going to nurse a sick friend," he answered, his brown eyes twinkling.

"I never said it was a *lady* friend, though, did I?"

Rana's lips had parted in speechless surprise. Ruby went back to studying her menu. Trent boomed out a laugh that attracted the attention of several diners, who then recognized him and came over to their table to ask for his autograph.

Since then Rana had ceased to be self-conscious about her affair with Trent in front of his aunt. Ruby acted as though there was nothing peculiar about the handsome, charismatic "hunk" falling head over heels in love with the "frump." But Rana wasn't so naive as to think that other people wouldn't find his attraction to her strange.

The moment she entered the parlor and saw Tom Tandy's expression, she realized just what an odd pair they made in the eyes of the world. Rana and Trent Gamblin would have been a golden couple, but Miss Ramsey had no place at his side. If she hadn't known that before, the football player's reaction spelled it out clearly. To say that he was shocked was putting it mildly.

His lantern jaw dropped open and his mouth went slack with astonishment. Rana actually felt sorry for him. Trent had no doubt painted a word picture of her for the young man, and Miss Ramsey was hardly what he had expected.

"Tom, this is Ana Ramsey. Ana, Tom Tandy."

"How do you do, Tom," she said, extending her hand. It was still rough and unmanicured, though she had recently wanted to let her nails grow out again just for the pleasure of scratching Trent's back with them. When he kissed her hands or held them tightly in his, which was frequently, she longed for the days when they had been pampered. Tom briefly gripped her hand before releasing it. "Please sit down. I see that Trent has already gotten you something to drink."

Whether Trent realized it or not, this was an awkward moment. She was playing gracious hostess in an effort to put the flabbergasted young man at ease. Now was the time for him to say to his buddy, "She's as beautiful as you described," or "I can see now why you've tucked yourself away down here in Galveston, you sly thing, you."

Instead, Tom just stared at Rana. It wasn't out of recognition. He was simply dismayed, she guessed, over her dissimilarity to all of Trent's former girlfriends.

"Would you like another beer?" she asked.

"No. No, thank you," Tom said, lowering his tall, muscular frame back onto Ruby's antique sofa. The Victorian furniture hadn't been designed to seat professional football players comfortably. He sank into the deep cushions, and his knees came up almost level with his chest. If Rana could have joked at that moment, she might have remarked on how ridiculously out of place Tom and Trent looked in the parlor, like giants in a dollhouse.

"Do you want a beer, darling?" Trent asked as he pulled Rana down beside him on the love seat.

"You know I can't stand the stuff, but I'll take a sip of yours just for something wet. It's so hot out."

She took a sip from his can of cold beer and licked her lips. He smiled, kissed her quickly, and then looked at Tom as though for approval. Tom just continued to gape.

"Are you staying for dinner, Tom?" Rana asked to break an uncomfortable silence.

"Uh, no." He cleared his throat loudly when his voice came out as little more than a croak. "I've, uh, got to get back. I have a . . . uh . . . date."

He had driven to Galveston with the hope of taking Trent back to Houston with him. He figured that his friend had been playing monk long enough. They were due to leave for summer training camp in a few days. Tom intended to party between now and then, and he had assumed Trent would be thinking along the same lines. It had been shocking enough to learn that Trent had no intention of carousing.

But when Ana Ramsey had walked into the room, Tom felt as if the rug had been jerked out from under him. He couldn't believe his eyes. Any moment now, he thought, somebody was going to tell him the punch line.

"I think Trent's visit down here has done wonders for him," Tom said conversationally.

If Trent's Ana had been beautiful and sophisticated, he would have had no trouble bantering with her. But this woman in the baggy trousers and vest left him tongue-tied. "He's in better shape than I've seen him in in years," he said.

"We've been worried about his shoulder, but when he went to see the doctor last week, he pronounced it completely healed." She turned to Trent and smiled.

"So Trent says."

"I think he can lead the Mustangs to the Super Bowl this year and win," Rana said confidently. She laid her hand on Trent's thigh in one of those unplanned gestures that says so much about the level of intimacy in a relationship.

Trent emitted an exaggerated sigh and stretched his arms out along the back of the love seat. "The lady adores me," he said expansively.

Rana socked him playfully in the stomach. They engaged in a skirmish of batting hands that resulted in an affectionate hug.

"Trent tells me you paint, or something," Tom said to Rana when they finally settled down.

"More like 'or something.' I paint on clothing, but I'm diversifying. I'm thinking of going into upholstery—sofa cushions and accent pillows, that sort of thing."

Tom nodded, but she didn't think he had any concept of what she was talking about. Barry had suggested that if the wealthy women of Houston were willing to spend hundreds on original hand-painted clothing, they might be just as willing to pay thousands to have an original hand-painted chair or chaise or sofa. Rana had given it careful thought and then had bounced the idea off Trent. He had given it his wholehearted endorsement.

"Do some up," he had suggested. "To see how they catch on, we could place them in a few of the prime properties my company is handling."

"That's where I've been today," Rana told Tom now. "I went to a textile-surplus warehouse to buy fabric." She indicated the large package she had left in the doorway when Trent escorted her into the parlor. "Speaking of which," she said as she stood up, "I'll excuse myself to go upstairs and get to work."

"Can't you relax and visit awhile longer?" Trent said, catching her arm.

"I'm sure you and Tom have a lot to talk about, so I'll leave you alone. It was nice to meet you, Tom."

He stood up, shuffling his feet awkwardly. "Likewise."

"See you later, darling." Trent tugged on her wrist and pulled her down for a lengthy kiss. When she straightened back up, she nodded self-consciously at Tom. After retrieving her package she went upstairs.

Trent watched her go, a smile on his lips. He was remembering last night. His loins stirred with the memory of how good her hair felt brushing against his thighs. Once she was out of sight, he turned back to Tom, who was sitting with his big feet spread wide, staring at the floor between them.

"Well, what do you think?" Trent asked, taking a long pull on his can of beer.

Tom twiddled his thumbs, cleared his throat, rolled his shoulders, blew out a gust of air, and finally raised his head. "I think you're probably the cruelest, coldest, most self-centered sonofabitch I've ever known."

Trent slowly lowered the can of beer. He kept his eyes riveted on Tom as he set it on the coffee table. They stared at each other for a long moment; then Trent laughed shortly. "Any particular reason why?"

Tom stood up and began prowling the room with a notable absence of grace. On the football field he could make impossible catches, leaping between three defenders to come up with the football. But now, he bumped into a tea table, upset a scrimshaw sculpture, and caught his toe in the corner of the rug. Finally, he made it across the obstacle course of the parlor to the window.

"For what you're doing to this woman," he said in a low voice.

"What I'm doing to this woman has brought each of us a tremendous amount of pleasure. Not that it's any of your damn business," Trent said tightly.

Tom turned around abruptly, controlling his temper only a trifle more successfully than Trent. "You asked my opinion, remember? All right, you're going to get it. I think the way you're manipulating this woman is beneath even you, Trent."

" 'Even me'?"

"Yeah, even you. I've seen you break dozens of female hearts. But most of the women you've dumped could take it. They had other interests. They had a lot of things going for them. Looks. Plenty of money. And other guys waiting in the wings. I'm not sure this woman can survive you."

"I hate to keep repeating you, but 'survive'?"

"What happens to her when you go off to summer camp?"

"She stays here. She sure as hell can't go and bunk with

me. What happens to team wives when the married guys leave for summer camp or travel during the season? I don't get your drift, Tom."

"Then I'll be more specific. What happens to her when you return from training camp, move back into your Houston house, and resume your old lifestyle?"

"Once the season starts, my time won't be my own. My job will cut our time together. Don't you think I realize that?"

"Then you intend to go on seeing her?"

"Yes, dammit. What did you think?"

"You intend to make her part of your life in Houston?"

"Yes."

Tom shook his head in bafflement. "And do you honestly think she'll fit in? That she'll feel comfortable with your circle of friends?"

"Why shouldn't she?"

"*Why?* Aw, come on, Gamblin. I'm your best friend. You don't have to pull this dumb act with me. Look at her," he cried, pointing toward the stairs. "Does she look like the women you usually romance?"

Trent went rigid with fury. His powerful hands balled into fists at his sides. "I think you'd better leave."

"Like hell I will. I'm not saying this to hurt your feelings. I'm only pointing out what is already so plainly obvious in order to spare her a broken heart. Believe me, my sympathies are all with her."

"Well, thank you very much, but she doesn't need your sympathies. And just what is it that's so plainly obvious to you?"

"That you're using this woman to salve your ego, just as you've used this time away to heal your shoulder. She's just what you needed. As you said yourself, the lady adores you. It's apparent from the way she looks at you. It would be easy for any woman to fall for you, Trent. Hell, I'm a man, and I'm straight, but do you think I'm blind? You're handsome. You're a hunk. You're a superstar in the sports world, and according to all reports I've heard—usually from women crying their hearts out over you—you're a superstud in bed. What woman wouldn't fall in love with you? Any man would envy the luck you have with women, but I think you're a real bastard for taking advantage of it with this lady."

Trent placed his hands on his hips and tilted his head back in a challenging stance. "And just how am I doing that, Mr. Psychology Professor?" he asked, prodding his friend where he knew it would hurt the most. Tom Tandy had majored in psychology and had even earned a doctorate. But he felt that a "dumb jock" wouldn't have much credibility in that field, so he had given up his dream to actually practice.

Tom, rocking on the balls of his feet in an effort to stem his anger, answered calmly. He raised his large hands and began ticking off examples on his fingers. "In the last year you've squired a campus queen from the University of

Texas whose daddy owns practically all of downtown Fort Worth; a young widow who controls not only her late husband's cattle empire, but the minds of the social set in West Texas; a woman who chairs a bank in Corpus Christi; and a princess whose royal father is living out the rest of his life in this country in exile. Shall I go on?"

Trent crossed his arms on his chest. "Please do, and get to the point."

"The point is that in each instance, your relationship with the woman rocked along fine . . . as long as you were winning. You lose a football game, and zip, the love affair is off. Zilch. *Finis.*"

Trent shifted uncomfortably and turned his back on Tom, ostensibly to straighten an ashtray on the coffee table. "So I get moody after a loss. So?"

"Uh-uh. It's more than moodiness, my friend. You have to be top dog in the relationship. The star. You don't want your woman to outshine you in any shape, form, or fashion.

"You're a natural competitor on the playing field and in business, and you always play fair. You actually enjoy the challenge. But your love life is one arena where you can't stand competition. A beautiful or famous or talented or successful woman poses a threat to your ego, especially when you're losing football games . . . or suffering from a shoulder injury that might end your career." Tom came nearer and spoke softly, almost compassionately. "Ana Ramsey poses no such threat, does she, Trent?"

Trent spun around, his jaw grinding with anger, but

Tom wasn't intimidated. He went on undaunted. "She's not as good-looking as you. She certainly doesn't outdress you. She doesn't outrank you in the finance department. I'm sure she's talented, but you're the unqualified star this time, aren't you?"

He drew a deep sigh and laid his hand on Trent's shoulder. "She was just what you needed a couple of weeks ago, a woman who adored you and who accepted your every word as gospel, who thought you could do no wrong. You represented Prince Charming to her. Let's face facts, Trent. When you came here, you were on a losing streak. You've used Ana to pump up your deflated ego."

Trent's anger had dissipated, because some of what Tom had said was right. He liked and respected Tom Tandy both as an athlete and as a human being. Their friendship went back for years, and he supposed that fact gave Tom the freedom to speak candidly.

"On some points you're right, Tom. But you're wrong about what I feel for Ana. Initially it was just as you say; I was out for a lark. She was convenient. So why not take advantage? I had nothing better to do." He peered straight into his friend's eyes. "But for the first time in my life, I came to really know a woman. It sounds sappy, but I love her. I know she's different. That's what I love about her."

Tom searched Trent's face for a long while, weighing his sincerity. Then his ugly features stretched into an embarrassed smile. "Then I've been way out of line. I hope it all works out. Friends?" he asked, sticking out his hand.

Trent grasped it warmly and slapped Tom's shoulder. "Friends."

Tom left shortly after that. Trent bounded up the stairs shouting Ana's name. "Where's the fire?" she asked, poking her head out the door.

"Right here." He backed her into the room, shut the door with a tap of his foot, wrapped her in his arms, and branded her mouth with a kiss. "I want to make love."

"Trent," she said with a light laugh, and tried to wiggle out of his embrace.

"Now."

"I'm right in the middle of—"

He kissed her again and touched her knowingly. They were so familiar with each other by now that he knew what she responded to. The fire he spoke of spread into her, and was fueled by her never-ending desire for him.

Clothes were discarded hastily. They knelt together on the floor. His mouth kissed its way down her throat to her breasts. Her back arched over his supporting arms and her heavy hair swung free. Undisciplined, his tongue caressed her nipples until they were taut and dewy. Then he eased her back, positioned her for maximum sensation, and entered her.

Even after it was over, he lay nestled inside her, breathing the floral scent of her hair. It was already growing dusky outside, but he could see her well enough to wonder why Tom didn't find her as beautiful as he did. Her hair was thick and silky as it spread out behind her head on the floor. Her skin, bathed with a sheen of perspiration from their vigorous lovemaking, seemed to glow in the diminishing light.

He stayed sheathed inside her until he was ready to love her again. This time he went slowly, savoring each precious moment, each delicious sound she made in response to his stroking.

No other woman had ever pleased him so well. All through the evening, he proved his delight in her repeatedly and denied everything that Tom had said. Especially to himself.

Nine

At first Rana couldn't remember why she didn't want to wake up. Then it came to her, and she squeezed her eyes shut again.

Trent was leaving today.

Rolling onto her back, she stared at the ceiling over her bed and wondered if she would be able to handle his departure with dignity. Before she could think about it long, however, there was a discreet knock on her door. She scrambled from the bed and rushed across the room to open the door a crack.

"I wouldn't have to come tiptoeing across the hall at six A.M. if you'd let me spend the night in your bed. But I love you anyway." Trent leaned forward and kissed her gently. Ruby knew about their affair, but Rana had remained steadfast about their need for some privacy from each other. She had stubbornly refused to sleep with him for the entire night. "Why aren't you dressed to run?"

"I didn't know you'd want to," she whispered back.

"I do. This is our last morning to jog together on the Galveston beach. At least for a while." He reached behind her and patted her bottom. "Hurry. I'll be warming up on the front lawn."

So he was going to pretend that today was just like any other . . . at least for a few hours.

When they returned from an exhilarating workout, they drank fruit juice and ate a light breakfast in the kitchen, as had become their habit. But when they were climbing the stairs, he took her hand and pulled her into his room, closing and locking the door behind them.

"What are you doing?" she asked.

"Locking you in. Today we shower together."

That had been another intimacy she had refused him. "Trent, you know how—"

He laid a finger over her lips. "No arguments. Consider this your send-off to a soldier on his way to the front."

"But—"

"Do you love me?"

He asked the question with such intensity that she dared not make light of it. "Yes," she said truthfully. "I love you, Trent."

"And I love you. We've been as intimate as a man and woman can be. I've touched you, kissed you, everywhere. But I want to *see* you in the light. Do this for me. Please."

He was the first—and probably would be the last—person ever to love her just as she was. Could she deny him anything on their final day together? She didn't protest when he began removing her ugly gray sweat suit. She let him peel away one shapeless garment after another until she stood before him naked.

Several minutes ticked by before he said anything. His eyes traveled from the crown of her head to her feet, back up, then down again with more leisure. Bewildered, he hissed a soft curse.

"Why do you dress the way you do? You've got one of the most spectacular bodies I've ever seen. I don't understand," he said hoarsely, shaking his head in confusion.

Rana wanted to weep with happiness. His compliment meant more to her than any she had ever received. Words to the same effect had been repeated to her so often that they had lost their meaning. But Trent's speaking of them gave those words new significance.

If she let herself dwell on it, she would cry, and if she began, she was afraid she would never stop. This was too precious a day to waste on tears. So she closed the distance between them and, standing on tiptoe, murmured against his lips. "You're wearing too many clothes, Mr. Gamblin." She began working his shorts down his hips.

Before they stepped into the shower stall, he snatched off her glasses. She reached for them reflexively, but he held them far above her head. She turned her face aside.

"Ana, look at me."

She loved him, didn't she? If he did recognize her, would it matter so much now? He would leave her in a few hours anyway. Gradually her head came around, until she was staring up at him.

He seemed to lose himself in the swirling depths of her eyes. "Such an unusual color," he remarked distantly, as though talking to himself. "It's a crime for you to hide such beautiful eyes behind these tinted lenses."

He put the glasses on the edge of the sink, then cupped her face between his hands and dotted it with soft kisses. He kissed her closed eyelids and her cheeks, her forehead and her chin, before settling his warm, open mouth over hers and sending his tongue deep into it.

Their shower together became a ritual of love. Lips sipped water from pulsing flesh, unashamed and uninhibited. Soapy hands explored slick skin, caressed and massaged, earned murmurs of pleasure and sighs of fulfillment. His lathered fingers moved provocatively through the silky tuft at the top of her thighs. Slippery hands made milking motions that left him gasping.

"You make me so hard," he rasped, bringing their bodies together. Their coupling was exquisite and seemingly timeless.

The water from the shower turned cool long before their ardor.

·　　·　　·

Lunch was a solemn occasion. Ruby was unnaturally glum. "Are you sure you haven't forgotten anything?"

"I've packed everything and checked the room twice, Auntie. If I've overlooked anything, you can send it to my house in Houston. The housekeeper will be there even if I'm not."

Rana said little. She was concentrating on not bursting into tears, while she idly moved the unwanted chicken salad around on her plate.

"What time is your flight?" Ruby asked.

"We're scheduled to take off at four, but I'm sure media interviews will delay us. They always do." A frown creased his brow as he watched Ana. He had expected a little show of sadness on her part, since they wouldn't be seeing each other for three weeks. He hadn't thought she would be this despondent.

"Will you be interviewed on camera?" Ruby asked him.

"Maybe. Watch the news tonight and you might see me." Trying to lighten the mood around the dining table, he winked at his aunt. "Should I wave to you?"

When they had dragged out lunch as long as they possibly could, all that was left to do was say good-bye. Trent hugged his aunt and gave her a smack on the lips. "*I* thank you, the *coach* thanks you, the *team* thanks you, the *fans* thank you."

She pretended to be irritated. "What are you blabbering about, you silly boy?"

"If you hadn't given me a quiet room to rest in and three square meals a day, I wouldn't be in such terrific condition. All the other guys will have a much harder time at camp than I will, and I owe it all to your tender, loving care."

Ruby blotted her damp eyes with a hanky and mumbled that he had an open invitation to come and stay any time. He would always be welcome at her house. After his promise to call her often, she discreetly withdrew, leaving him alone in the entrance hall with Rana. He had loaded his belongings in his car before lunch. It was waiting for him at the curb.

Without a word, he pulled Rana into his arms. She buried her face in his neck and locked her hands together at the small of his back. She wished she could gather his strength, his smell, his warmth, and cork them in a bottle to be enjoyed later whenever she needed a "fix" of Trent.

"Are you going to tell me?" he asked softly, stroking her hair.

"Tell you what?"

"Why you look like someone has just run over your kitty."

She smiled tremulously. "Is that what I look like?"

"Or worse."

"I'm sad. I hate to see you go."

"It's only for three weeks."

It's for a lifetime.

"I'll call every night."

For a few nights, then you'll skip a night, and then another.
"I'm going to miss you. So damn much."
Until you meet someone else.

He tilted her head back and kissed her. Knowing that this would be the last time she ever felt his lips on hers, she poured all her love for him into that kiss.

When he pulled back, he let his thumb glide over her lips. "Kiss me like that a few more times, and I'll be able to fly to California under my own power." He hugged her quickly, fiercely. "See you in three weeks."

Then he was gone.

She groped her way to the deacon's bench behind the stairs and collapsed on it. She began to cry. Bitterly. Rackingly. And this time he wasn't there to lend her comfort.

At least Rana's days were busy. She finished her outstanding orders in ten days. Barry had promoted his idea of hand-painted upholstery fabric. She already had an order for three oversized cushions to decorate a poolside wicker settee.

To her delight, Trent called faithfully every night, and they talked until Tom, his roommate, demanded that he shut up and turn out the lights. He phoned with such regularity that it was with some surprise that Ruby called Rana to the phone one evening and said, "It's a man, but it's not Trent. And whoever it is, he got your name wrong. He pronounced it Rana."

She avoided Ruby's questioning eyes as she took the receiver from her. "Hello?"

"Rana Ramsey?"

A quick glance assured her that Ruby had already become engrossed in her television serial. "This is she."

The caller identified himself as a representative of a life-insurance firm in New York City. "You are the beneficiary of a fifty-thousand-dollar policy, and I wanted to verify your current address. You'll be receiving a check in the full amount, as the taxes were taken care of when the will was probated."

Her throat constricted. "Who . . . Who . . . ?"

"Oh, I'm sorry. Mr. Morey Fletcher."

Her knees almost buckled beneath her. She certainly didn't want to benefit financially from Morey's suicide. The thought made her nauseous. She swallowed hard, fought off the dizziness, and wet her lips. "But in instances such as his, I didn't think life-insurance policies were honored."

The man was obviously taken aback. "I'm sorry, I don't understand. What do you mean by 'instances such as his'?"

She couldn't bring herself to say the hateful word. "I mean, the way he died."

"The insurance company has found nothing irregular about Mr. Fletcher's death, Ms. Ramsey. No one could have predicted his reaction to the medication."

"Medication?" She virtually inhaled the word, making a wheezing sound.

"Yes, the drug to control blood pressure that his physician had prescribed for him. I apologize again. I thought you were acquainted with the circumstances of Mr. Fletcher's death."

"I thought I was too," Rana murmured. The implications of this telephone call were just beginning to sink in. Facing her mother's part in describing Morey's death was going to be painful.

"His doctor had given him a new prescription that day to bring his blood pressure down."

"I understood that he took the medication with alcohol."

"Yes, the postmortem confirmed the police report, but the alcohol content of his blood was so low as to be negligible. He might have had one glass of wine with dinner. Unfortunately, it's very difficult to prescribe the correct dosage of the drug he was taking, or to predict a patient's reaction to it. If someone else had been present when Mr. Fletcher lost consciousness, his life might have been saved, but the glass of wine made no difference one way or the other. I've upset you, Ms. Ramsey. Forgive me," he said when he heard her telltale sniffling.

"No, no, thank you. Thank you for telling me."

Morey's death *had* been an accident!

He might have been disappointed about her decision not to sign a new contract, but she hadn't driven him to suicide. She would continue to grieve for him, but she no longer had to bear the burden of responsibility for his death.

Her heart was still soaring when Trent called later that night. She told him about her previous call. "You can't imagine how relieved I feel, knowing that he didn't die hating me." Trent didn't know that Morey had been her agent, merely that he'd been a very dear friend.

"I was never convinced of that, darling." He let the contemplative moment pass, and then said, "Since you're in such high spirits, I'll ask you tonight."

"Ask me what?"

"Will you go to the preseason party with me?"

She clutched the receiver tightly. "The preseason party?"

"Yeah, the owners of the team throw a big bash every year after training camp and before the first exhibition game. It's a dress-up affair, quite a shindig, and I want you to be my date."

"I don't think I can go, Trent," she said quickly.

"Why not? Stringing me along already? Aunt Ruby hasn't rented my apartment to a Robert Redford type, has she? You like blonds better? Okay, I'll bleach my hair."

"Stop! No, I'm not stringing you along. I just don't think a 'bash' sounds like me. Especially a dress-up one."

"Hey, relax. You'll be with me, and I'm a star." She could envision his lazy, crooked, conceited grin, and her heart twisted with love. What would all his friends and teammates think of dowdy Ana Ramsey? She remembered Tom Tandy's face when he'd first met her, and knew then that she would never subject Trent to that kind of embarrassment.

Nor would she break her resolve and go to the party as Rana. Trent would feel like a colossal fool, and she couldn't do that to him either, not when the most important football season of his career was pending. He was feeling like a Super Bowl quarterback now. She wouldn't do anything to imperil his regained confidence.

"We'll see," she said obliquely to postpone refusing him outright.

But she knew she would never attend that party.

"Mother!"

"Hello, Rana."

Rana stood in the doorway, staring at Ruby's guest, who was sitting with the elderly woman in the parlor. Rana's face drained of color.

"Your mother arrived half an hour ago, dear," Ruby said, trying valiantly to ignore the apparent antagonism between the two women. She had disliked Susan Ramsey on sight, and her initial impression hadn't improved when the woman insisted that her daughter's name was Rana instead of Ana.

Only inbred southern hospitality had compelled Ruby to invite Susan into the parlor and offer her tea while they waited for Ana, or *Rana*, to return from her errands. Ruby hadn't liked Susan's probing questions, either, and had answered them as evasively as possible. "Would you like tea, Ana, dear?"

"No, thank you, Ruby," Rana said, never taking her eyes off her mother, who did nothing to mask her disapproval of the flamboyantly dressed landlady, the house, and her daughter.

"Then I'll leave you two alone to visit."

She bustled out, patting Rana on the arm reassuringly and whispering, "Just call out if you need me," as she went past her.

"You look dreadful," Susan began without preamble. "Your face is sunburned."

"This is an island, Mother. I'm out in the sun frequently, and I love it."

Susan sniffed her disapproval. "This Ruby person tells me that you have a beau."

"Ruby told you no such thing," Rana said calmly. She sat down in a chair opposite her mother's, where Susan sat so erect that no part of her back touched the cushion. "You may have deviously gleaned enough information from her to come to that conclusion, but don't suggest that my friend gossiped about me. I know better. Just as I know how persuasive you can be, Mother."

Susan's only reaction to her daughter's show of spunk was a slight raising of one groomed brow. "Are you living here with a man?"

"No. But I fell in love with a man who lived here. He's gone now."

"So I hear. A football player." She laughed in ridicule. "You're behaving like a fool over a broad pair of shoulders.

I should have known that's what was keeping you away from where you were supposed to be."

"Trent had nothing to do with my decision not to return to work."

"Didn't he?"

"No."

"We are speaking of Trent Gamblin, aren't we?"

"Yes."

"From what I've read recently, his career is in a steep decline."

"He had a shoulder injury last season, but he's coming back this year better than ever."

"Rana, for heaven's sake, spare me your sickening adulation." She picked at a nonexistent speck on her skirt. "Where does this shabby little affair go from here?"

"I don't know. But be assured of one thing, Mother. It's none of your business," she said, emphasizing each word. Susan's face went taut. "I've got a new life. A new career. My business is doing well, and growing. If and when I return to modeling, it will be my decision and will have nothing whatsoever to do with you."

Rana leaned forward and whipped off her glasses, giving her mother a penetrating stare. "Why did you lead me to believe that Morey's death was a suicide?"

Susan's composure slipped another notch. "I didn't."

"Oh, yes, you did. There's just no limit to how far you'll go, is there? You'll do anything to get your way. I pity you, Mother. You must be awfully lonely."

Susan sprang to her feet. "Save your pity. I've managed to pull myself together since your desertion. I sold the penthouse, and I intend to keep every penny of the equity."

"Congratulations. It's yours. I always hated that mausoleum you mistakenly referred to as 'home.' "

Susan continued as though she hadn't been interrupted. "With careful financial counseling from a man I've met recently, I'll live comfortably without you, Rana. He has invited me to stay with him for a while. I've volunteered to help him work out some of his personal problems."

Rana smiled at that piece of news. Susan had found another life to manage. "That's wonderful, Mother. I hope you'll be happy."

"I will be. While you waste your life with some musclebound buffoon who carries a football down a field."

"I don't know if Trent and I have a future together. But at least I'll be directing the course of my life, not you."

"Does he know who you are?"

Rana's eyes clashed with her mother's. Susan smiled with smug triumph when she realized that she had scored a direct hit. "No?" she purred. "From his aunt I understand that he's a man with a fragile ego, especially where his career is concerned. He probably wouldn't take too kindly to your international fame, would he? Is that why you're keeping your true identity a secret?"

"No!"

"Well, it's really no concern of mine," she said airily. "My friend had business in Houston, so we only flew down for the day." She picked up her purse, stood, and walked toward the hall. "I must go, or I'll be late meeting him back at the airport. I wanted to give you one last chance to come back, but I won't interfere in your life again, Rana. If you choose to live in obscurity and poverty, that's up to you. By the way, when I moved from the penthouse, I boxed up all your things. I'm having them shipped to you. Use or dispose of them as you see fit. Good-bye."

Rana's heart tore in two. This was it. This was their final farewell. She couldn't believe that she and her mother were parting company so coldly, possibly never to see each other again. From all indications, Susan was washing her hands of her.

"Mother," she called out, her voice quavering. She took several quick steps forward, her arms extended. Susan turned around, but her posture remained unyielding. Rana forced herself to a halt, but didn't let her mother's aloof veneer stop her from speaking what she felt she must.

"You said I live in poverty, but you're wrong. I'm rich. Wealthier than I've ever been." She paused, desperately wanting to see a glimmer of understanding and warmth in her mother's emotionless eyes. "I've found real beauty. I've learned what it is to love. Trent taught me, though he didn't even know it. I thought I hated you, but I don't. I love you. Not because of what you are, but in spite of it.

That's what it's all about, you see? I love you, Mother, and I'm sorry you'll never know the joy—not *happiness*—but the joy that can come from loving."

She expected nothing. Nothing was what she got. Susan turned on her heel and stalked out.

"So are you or aren't you?"

"I—"

"You'll have to speak louder, honey. I'm calling from the locker room, and it's noisy as hell. Will you meet me at the party? I'm the only guy on the team who hasn't got a date. They'll never let me live that down. You wouldn't be that cruel, would you?"

Ever since Susan's visit Rana had been debating what she would do on this day. It had come to the eleventh hour, and still she had made no decision. The team had returned to Houston late the night before. The coach had scheduled an early-morning practice, so it had been impossible for Trent to drive to Galveston to see her. The party was due to start in a few hours. He had every right to expect Rana's answer as to whether she was going to meet him there or not.

Rana had spent hours of agonizing thought pondering the question. Her confrontation with Susan, heart-wrenching as it had been, had accomplished something. Her mother had inadvertently raised some vital points that had forced

Rana to think seriously about her love for Trent. And his for her. He had vowed his love before leaving Galveston and told her repeatedly how much he loved her each time he'd called. During their separation his devotion hadn't waned. Rana had expected never to see him again, but it was clear that Trent planned to make her very much a part of his life.

What it came down to was this: Did he love her for what she was or for what she wasn't? Would he love Rana as much as he loved Ana? She couldn't continue the disguise forever. She had come to that decision, at least. She was as much Rana as she was Ana. Living behind the mask of dowdiness was as much a lie as living behind Rana's glamorous makeup and clothes.

Love meant acceptance. Trent either loved her or he didn't. It would be a grueling test, but she had to put him through it. Otherwise there could be no future for them.

Of course, she would have to go through the test too. That would be the hardest part. That was what she didn't know if she could bear.

"Yes, I'll be there," she said quietly.

"Great! I'm sending a limo for you."

"No! Don't be crazy."

"I'm crazy in love. And when I see you, I can't be held accountable for my actions."

He didn't know the ironic significance of those words.

They said a hasty good-bye. Trancelike, Rana walked

into her bathroom. Looking directly into the mirror, she slowly lowered the blue-tinted eyeglasses. Lest she capitulate to her fears, she cracked the glasses against the side of the bathtub before dropping the pieces into the wastepaper basket. She shook back her hair and gathered it into a ponytail.

Then she reached into the cabinet over the sink and took out her makeup kit.

Ten

She looked spectacular.

The dress she wore had been specially designed for a fragrance commercial. It was white, and highly dramatic. When she had gone through the trunks her mother had shipped to her, she'd selected this dress to wear to the party because it was one of her favorites and so typically "Rana."

She had altered the side seams to accommodate her fuller figure, but the silky fabric still draped each curve of her body as though caressing it. The neckline, which left one shoulder bare, was banded by sparkling beadwork. She wore no ornaments except a pair of jeweled earrings as glittering as tiny chandeliers.

She had trimmed her hair herself and conditioned it. After half an hour in hot curlers she hung her head down and brushed it vigorously. When she flung her head back, her hair fell into a full mane that framed her face and rippled over her shoulders.

Her nails were still short, but she had manicured them carefully and polished them with a frosted coral shade that matched her lip gloss.

Her complexion glowed after the facial she had treated it to. The olive skin tone was deepened to an even richer hue by her tan. She hadn't lost her knack for applying makeup. The cosmetics weren't obvious, but the effect she deftly created was startling. With her hair full and brushed away from her face, her cheekbones were prominently displayed.

It was an exotic face that reminded one of a pagan priestess. Blatantly sensual. A face that had a love affair with any camera.

The limo cruised to a halt in front of the River Oaks mansion, where the party was being held. The chauffeur came around to help her out. Clutching her small white, rhinestone-studded bag, she accepted his extended hand. "Thank you," she said softly.

"My pleasure, Miss Ramsey. Have an enjoyable evening."

The summer twilight was warm and balmy, heavily scented with blooming gardenias and magnolias. But the soft, humid air was only one reason her skin felt damp. She was nervous.

Behind a temporary rope barricade, representatives of the media trampled a low boxwood hedge as they clamored for photographs of arriving Mustangs team members and guests.

Shoulders back, head straight, swan neck arched, Rana swept past them. Someone whistled. "Jeez, who does *she* belong to?" The speaker was a sports reporter. He didn't recognize her. But the society reporter standing next to him did.

"Hurry," she instructed her photographer excitedly. "Take some pictures. Quick, before she gets inside."

"Who is she?" asked the curious sports reporter.

"Rana, you fool. Don't you ever read anything but *Sports Illustrated?* Come to think of it, she was featured in their swimsuit edition a few years ago."

"Oh, yeah, I remember now. She's a famous model, isn't she?"

"The tops."

"What's she doing here?" he asked.

"I don't know, but I intend to find out. She hasn't been seen in public for months. The rumor was she'd gotten fat, or something."

"Every woman should be so fat," he said, leering.

Rana had overheard enough of the conversation to know that her cover was blown. The die was cast. Whatever the outcome, it was out of her hands now. She didn't care what anyone else thought or said about her. *How would Trent react?*

She glided up the front steps of the colonial-style house.

Standing just inside the front door was a distinguished-looking white-haired couple, whom Rana recognized as the owners of the Houston Mustangs football team. They were talking to Tom Tandy.

She paused for a moment before continuing forward. Tom saw her out of the corner of his eye. He did a double take. In typically male fashion, his eyes slid down, then back up.

"Hello, Tom," she said softly. Her voice was barely loud enough for him to hear over the loud music and raucous conversation.

His eyes swung up to hers. Stupefied, he responded with a mumbled, "Hi." He made room for her beside the team's owners, who were looking at her curiously and obviously awaiting an introduction.

"Mr. and Mrs. Harrison, I'd like you to meet, uh, Miss, uh, Ms. . . ."

It was apparent that Tom didn't recognize her, so she spared him further embarrassment. "I'm Rana," she said, extending her hand.

Mr. Harrison shook it, stunned speechless, as most men were upon meeting her for the first time. Mrs. Harrison, however, smiled graciously and said, "What an honor to have you in our home, Rana. That is a stunning dress."

"Thank you."

"Tom, why don't you get Rana something to drink?"

"Yeah, yeah, sure. You want to, uh . . ." He nodded toward the bar, indicating that she should move in that direction with him. He didn't touch her. She thanked the Harrisons for the party and left them to greet the other guests who were filing in. As he shouldered his way through the crowd, Tom stared at her in bewilderment, trying to figure out how this beautiful creature knew him. Why didn't he remember ever meeting her? He'd never been *that* drunk!

" 'Rana,' you say?"

"Yes, but I was introduced to you as Ana. In Galveston. A few weeks ago. Have you seen Trent? Is he here yet?"

Tom stopped dead in his tracks. His mouth fell open as though hinged at the jaw. He gripped Rana's shoulders in his large hands and stared down at her. "Well, I'll be damned." He repeated that several times, then threw back his head and howled with laughter. "That sonofa—. Wait till I get my hands on him. He's played some rotten jokes on me, but this one is the big granddaddy. That . . . that . . . Boy, did he ever put one over on me. And you too! You were in on it, right? Lord have mercy, I wouldn't have recognized you in a million years."

"It wasn't a joke, exactly. You see, I—"

She spotted Trent.

He was standing several yards away, chatting companionably with several of his teammates—linemen, if their size was any indication. They towered over Trent, but to Rana, he was the most impressive man in the room.

His dark hair was as carelessly styled as ever, curling over his ears and collar. His tanned face contrasted appealingly with his white shirt. Only Trent could get by with wearing such closely fitted white trousers. They were perfectly tailored to his narrow buttocks and trim thighs. The fit of his navy blazer was impeccable.

As he laughed, his teeth flashed brilliantly. His brown eyes, which kept glancing toward the front door, were shining with excitement and expectation.

Rana's heart ached with love for him. She wanted to continue staring at him for a long time, prolonging the inevitable. But it had to happen. Only seconds after she'd spotted him his eyes scanned the crowd and came to a stop on her.

Trent, like his friend before him, did a double take when he saw the dazzling woman in white. She had dark red hair, skin that looked as lustrous as marble and as delicious as a ripe peach, eyes that spoke volumes, and a figure that made him think she might not be real.

Feeling a sharp pang of guilt for the sudden pounding of his heart, he tore his eyes away from her. *Where was Ana?*

The woman's eyes compelled him to go back for one more look. She was still staring at him. He acknowledged her interest with a slight nod. Her lips parted in a hesitant smile. He noticed then that her front teeth overlapped a little, but they certainly didn't detract—

Rana knew the moment recognition dawned in Trent. She saw realization break across his face as visibly as ink spilled on white paper. Disbelief was the first expression she read there, then gladness. He even elbowed his way past a monstrous tackle and took a step toward her. She experienced one blissful moment of pure joy before the expression she had dreaded appeared on his features.

The wide smile, there only a fleeting second ago, disappeared abruptly. His eyes went from shining warmth to glittering coldness. Even his body changed. It became stiff and rigid, as though he had snapped to attention.

She watched him turn angrily on his heel and shove his way through the crowd. The partygoers around them, unaware of the drama unfolding in their midst, were still drinking, eating, celebrating.

"Say, I don't get it," Tom said as Rana set out after Trent. "What's wrong with him? What's going on?"

"We'll explain everything later, Tom."

"Do you want me to come along?"

"No. Thanks anyway, but we need to be alone," she said over her shoulder.

It only took that rapid glance behind her to lose sight of Trent. He had always seemed to tower over her, but he was dwarfed by most of his teammates. The athletes seemed as immovable as giant redwoods when Rana tried to wend her way through them. Her eyes frantically darted around the obstacles of their massive bodies.

She caught a glimpse of Trent going through a set of French doors on the far side of the room and struggled to push through the crowd. It didn't help when the dance band chose that moment to break into the team's theme song. Drunk on champagne and optimism about the forthcoming season, everyone went a little crazy.

She finally made it through the gyrating throng to the French doors, and stepped outside into the sultry evening. Steps led down to a brick patio and a magnificent pool. A pair of lovers was unabashedly necking on a chaise. Trent was angrily striding around the far end of the pool, furiously grappling with the knot of his necktie.

"Trent, wait!"

Either he didn't hear her or he was ignoring her cry. She feared the latter and went running down the steps after him. Her progress was impeded by her high heels and narrow skirt. She kicked off her shoes and hiked the skirt of her dress above her knees.

The bricks were hot. By contrast, the grass was cool and damp on her bare feet as she followed Trent's progress across the lawn toward the man-made lake. A white summerhouse with lacy gingerbread trim stood on its ferny banks.

It was there that Rana caught up with Trent. He was in the act of slinging off his blazer and throwing it into a wicker chair. His necktie lay looped around his neck, and his shirt was unbuttoned almost to his waist. His impressive, hair-matted chest was heaving with rage.

He launched his verbal attack the moment she stepped into the opening of the gazebo. "Did you come to see if my ears were growing?"

Baffled by his question, she shook her head. Until then she hadn't realized that she was crying. Tears splashed against her cheeks. "What? What do you mean?"

"You made a jackass out of me. I presume you came to see if I could actually bray."

"It's not like that, Trent."

Belligerently he propped his hands on his hips. "No? Then what *is* it like? Huh? At least have the courtesy to tell me why you made a fool of me."

"Making a fool of you wasn't my intention. You moved in on me, not the other way around. Remember? Who pursued whom first?"

He looked down at the index finger that was pointing at him imperiously. He didn't recognize it as the one often smudged with paint. The eyes that gazed into his in the darkness were exquisite. And unrecognizable as well. His anger was momentarily overridden by bafflement. "Who the hell are you?"

"My name is Rana."

"I know that," he said irritably. "I'm not your average dumb jock, though you obviously seem to think so. I read magazines. I drive down the highway, for heaven's sake." He made an angry, sweeping gesture with his hand. "Who could miss you sprawled across a billboard half naked? I watch TV. I see the inane talk shows that focus on the really important things, like hem lengths, while half the world is starving."

"Oh," she ground out, "and I suppose a football game has much more global merit."

He put his face in his hands for a moment, trying to cap his erupting temper. "You're right. Neither one of us amounts to much, do we? The thing that galls me is that I make no bones about my shallowness. You, on the other hand . . . What was the disguise for? Those damn clothes and all the rest?"

"I left modeling behind me more than six months ago. I got fed up with it."

"With looking great? With having the world at your feet, with every woman in the world trying to copy your look? Come on, Ana, or Rana, or whatever the hell your name is, I wasn't born yesterday. Give me a reason that's at least plausible enough to believe."

"It wasn't the career I left behind. It was everything that went with it."

"Yeah," he said sarcastically, "like fame and fortune."

"My mother was trying to sell me to a rich old man," she said heatedly. "Is that plausible enough for you? I chose not to prostitute myself that way, and left New York. I came here, moved in with Ruby. I wanted a new name. An unrecognizable, plain, ordinary face. Anonymity. Peace. I wanted people to accept me without the glamorous trimmings, to see past the surface, into the woman I am on the inside."

"Okay, I'll buy that for now." His eyes took in the hairdo, the dress, the accessories. "But what about tonight? Why, after having made that drastic change, did you show up like this tonight?"

She took a step toward him. "I fell in love, Trent. With you."

He turned his back and shoved his hands into his pockets. He stared out over the still lake. Not a breath of air stirred. It was suffocatingly muggy. Crickets whirred from the trees lining the lake and bullfrogs croaked from cool, muddy hideouts. The music from the party seemed even farther away than it was, as though it couldn't quite penetrate the heavy air.

"What has that got to do with anything?" he asked after a tense, lengthy silence.

"Everything. You said you love me. *Me*," she stressed, pressing her hand over her breasts. "Well, this is a part of me. Up until a few months ago it was a vital part."

"How do I know your love for me isn't as phony as the rest of you?" He came around to face her again.

His accusing glare made her angry. "What was phony about Ana Ramsey?"

"Her name, for one thing," he said, punctuating his outburst with a jabbing finger.

"*You* assumed my name was Ana because you saw 'Ana R.' on the paintings. That's Rana spelled backward, in case you haven't noticed."

"Very clever," he said snidely. "Why didn't you correct me?"

She knotted her fingers together at her waist. "I was still afraid of discovery. I didn't have it all sorted out yet. I needed more time."

"You've had time since then. Plenty of time."

"But when would it have been right to tell you, Trent? You were falling in love with me, and I wanted you to." A tear rolled down her cheek. It didn't spoil her beauty. It was as crystal-clear and sparkling as the jewels that dangled from her ears. "You were the first person in my life to like me, then to love me, for what I was, not for what I looked like. I couldn't bring myself to risk losing that. Forgive me for deceiving you."

She shuddered as she drew in an unsteady breath. "You're angry, and you have every reason to be. I knew you would be, when I came here tonight. But I never intended to make a fool of you. I didn't enjoy tricking you all those weeks. There were times I wanted to tell you, but you said you loved me because I was different. I wasn't certain you'd love Rana as you did Ana."

She blotted the tears off her cheeks and laughed softly. "After our first night together, I wanted to put on makeup, to dress up. I wanted to be beautiful for you, just as any woman wants to be beautiful in the eyes of her lover. But the things you said to me, your touch, made me feel beautiful. More beautiful than I've ever felt. And it had nothing to do with what I looked like.

"For you to understand my motives, you would have to know the loneliness this face"—she pointed a finger toward her chin—"has caused me all my life. I won't belabor the point, because you might think, 'What is she complaining about? Her face has made her a fortune. She's beautiful.' But I've known the same kind of cruel discrimination an unattractive woman is subjected to. Prejudice, rejection, alienation, hurt, no matter what the reason."

She moved to stand close to him and bravely laid her hand on his chest. "You loved Ana in spite of her plainness. I'm the same woman, Trent. Can you love me—more than that, can you *accept* me—if I wear this face?"

His eyes were embarrassingly moist, and he blinked in an effort not to disgrace himself. "You are so beautiful," he said hoarsely. "I don't . . . I don't know you. You're like something out of mythology, a goddess."

"But I'm not, Trent. Talk to me," she pleaded. "Touch me. Kiss me and you'll know I'm the very same."

She met him more than halfway. He didn't do much more than incline his head toward her before she flung her arms around him. She rested her head on his chest and held him close.

"I missed you," she whispered, nuzzling her face in the opening of his shirt. Her breath feathered through his chest hair. She kissed his tanned skin. "I missed you."

He groaned softly and pulled the familiar body closer to him. His fingers sank into her hair, and he tilted her head back for his kiss. But a second before their lips met, he hesitated.

She gripped handfuls of his hair and pulled him down nearer. "Don't you dare become a coward now. Don't you dare be afraid to mess me up. Kiss me just as you always have."

That invitation was the only one he needed. His lips slanted hard and hungrily over hers. They parted eagerly. He thrust his tongue inside her mouth and made fervent love to it. Her arms locked around his neck possessively. She arched up against him, adjusting her body to complement his.

Then he knew. She was his. He was home.

"What did Aunt Ruby think?"

"Poor dear. For once, she was speechless."

"She recognized Rana?"

"Oh, yes. You know her and her fashion magazines. She had heard my mother call me Rana and—"

"Your mother? When?"

"I had a surprise visit from her. I found out that Morey—"

"Who's Morey?"

"My agent. My friend who died."

"The one you thought was a suicide?"

"Yes, because that was what my mother had led me to believe."

"What a *bitch*."

"Yes, well . . ."

"I'm sorry for the interruptions. Go ahead. This is all so confusing."

"I'll fill in the blanks later. Suffice it to say that Mother came to see me and it wasn't a happy reunion." Her voice took on a sad tone. "I hope that someday she and I will reach an understanding and feel some affection for each other."

Trent kissed her temple gently. "I hope so, too, but only for your sake. Anyway, back to Aunt Ruby."

"She had actually heard two people call me Rana, but apparently the name didn't sink in. When I came downstairs tonight, she just stared and started sputtering. I told her I'd explain everything later."

"It seems that you've got a lot of explaining to do, Miss Ramsey," he said, lifting her chin with his finger.

"Yes. But as I said . . . later."

He pulled her over him and laced his fingers together on the back of her head. Their kiss was lengthy and intimate and erotic.

They hadn't stayed at the party long after their reconciliation. After some tempestuous kissing in the gazebo, they had repaired their clothes and retrieved Rana's shoes before returning to the house. Tom met them on the patio, looking worried and confused.

"What the hell is going on?" he demanded.

They invited him to join them as they went through the sumptuous buffet line. Over supper they gave him a brief rundown of the facts. Tom shook his head in aggravation. "I might have known that Gamblin, my buddy the superstud, would end up with the most gorgeous woman in the whole U.S. of A.," he grumbled.

"Are you really a 'superstud'?" Rana asked him now, latching onto his earlobe with her teeth. They were lying entwined, naked, in his king-size bed. After a cursory tour of his house and a terse good night to the hovering house-keeper, Trent had taken her straight to bed.

"Complaining?" He cupped her hips with his hard, strong fingers and held her in place.

"Uh-uh." She sighed, rocking against him. "But I'm a monogamous creature, Trent."

His eyes locked with hers. "So am I. Now."

She traced his mouth with her fingertip. "Do we have a future together?"

"We do if you'll have a broken-down football player for a husband."

She lifted his right hand to her mouth and kissed the crooked fingers. "I want you for my husband more than anything in the world. But you're far from broken down."

"I'm serious, Rana." The name came easily to him now. "This season I might get out there on the field and make a laughingstock of myself from Green Bay to Miami."

"You won't," she whispered fiercely. "But if you don't win a single game, it won't be the end of the world. Don't you know by now what a tremendous success you are?"

"I am?"

"At the things that are really important."

"Such as?"

"Such as being a loving, caring human being."

"You don't think I'm manipulative? Tom accused me of falling in love with 'Ana' solely because you were the first woman who didn't threaten my fragile ego."

She denied that theory with a shake of her head. "I disagree with him, but maybe I helped teach you something."

"And what was that?"

"That all any of us has to give is our best. If we do that, we succeed, no matter what the outcome."

"I have learned that. But you've got to promise not to scold when I get moody and sullen after losing a game."

She kissed him. "I'll just have to think of ways to improve your bad moods, won't I?"

He angled his head to one side, and his eyes shone with a teasing light. "You know, I was a trifle jealous when those photographers clustered around us tonight as we left the party. They were as eager to get pictures of you as they were of me. Will you ever want to go back to modeling?"

"Maybe, but only if it doesn't conflict with you and the children."

His mouth slanted into that sly grin she loved. His eyebrow tipped down toward it. "Children?"

"Do you mind?"

"Hell, no. I've always had a hankering to fill up this house with a few kids."

"Good. Because I want to get started right away!"

He laughed and hugged her tightly. "God, you're gorgeous." He proudly surveyed her face. "I'd like to see you in action, preening before a camera or strutting down a runway with a spotlight on your hair." He ran his hands through it and she smiled.

"I'll have to lose some weight first."

"Lose some weight! You're all bones now."

"Not nearly bony enough to strut down a runway. But now that I've acquired a taste for potatoes and gravy, I don't know that I'll ever go back to a diet of lettuce and water."

"Just don't lose these," he said, lifting his head to kiss her breasts. "They're perfect."

She sighed as his mouth moved over her, then adjusted her body to his and took him inside her. He filled her with a warm, solid pressure.

"That's beautiful," he said with a groan.

"What?"

"That little sound you make every time I'm inside you. I want to hear it every day, at least once, for the rest of my life."

"Then you plan on keeping me?"

"I guess I will."

"Don't sound so self-sacrificing."

"Well, I do feel a little sorry for you."

"You do?"

"Yeah." He moaned with extreme pleasure when she

made a rolling motion with her hips. "If I don't marry you, you might end up an old maid."

"Why?" she asked on a soft gasp as he drove deeper.

"Because, you poor, homely thing, your front teeth are crooked."

Then he kissed her and heaven rained down.

About the Author

SANDRA BROWN began her writing career in 1980. After selling her first book, she wrote a succession of romance novels under several pseudonyms, most of which remain in print. She has become one of the country's most popular novelists, earning the notice of Hollywood and of critics. More than forty of her books have appeared on the *New York Times* best-seller list. There are fifty million copies of her books in print, and her work has been translated into twenty-nine languages. Prior to writing, she worked in commercial television as an on-air personality for *PM Magazine* and local news in Dallas. The parents of two, she and her husband now divide their time between homes in Texas and South Carolina.